Debi Eva

# THE SECRET SOCIETY
## OF
# DRAGON PROTECTORS

## 'The Cor Stan'

*Debi Evans*

**Published by Debi Evans & John MacPherson**

Cover design / illustration and chapter illustrations by John MacPherson

Published by Debi Evans & John MacPherson
Printed by Express Printing Services (L.L.C.)

ISBN   978-0-9554661-1-3

Books by
*Debi Evans & John MacPherson*
*In*

# THE SECRET SOCIETY

## OF

# DRAGON PROTECTORS

Series

'The Dragon's Tale'
'The Cor Stan'

# Contents

For Eleanor and Graham who have to put up with
dragons on a daily basis, and for our fans who
have embraced the SSDP so wholeheartedly.

## Chapter 1

# 'Unusual Dreams'

Angus sauntered along Piggleston High Street and as he did so he watched his breath mist in front of his face. Anyone who cared enough to observe, would see a lad walking with all the gracelessness of a typical twelve-year-old whose limbs were growing too quickly for the rest of his body. This awkwardness was somehow offset by the self assured expression on his face, for this boy had a huge secret.

It was a crisp, cold February day, the sun tried to shine but it was weak, watery and barely a token gesture to the day. Trees were dripping onto the pavement and there was no colour in the High Street, everything had a uniform greyness about it. The ground was still frosty from the night before which made it wet underfoot.

Like most lads his age Angus was just becoming aware of his appearance. As he passed each shop he would glance to the side and check his reflection in the window. His baggy jeans were fashionably too long, frayed at the bottom and wet from the bone chilling dampness. The laces on his trainers were barely done up and so his progress was more of a shuffle than a walk.

Angus recalled when he had first walked up this street last summer. Back then he could never have imagined what awaited him or what adventures he would have. He had made a new friend. One who was not only very special and secret, but someone he had sworn to protect at all costs. He remembered the first time they had flown together and how awesome the experience had been. At the time he was scared, no doubt about that, but he would never have passed up that chance. No-one else in the world knew what Angus was. Not the people in the street, nor his Mum and Dad. No-one that is, except the other protectors. His face was almost obscured by his hood, which was zipped right up to his nose. He pushed it down to see where he was and focused on his destination, Mrs James's sweet shop where the old children's ride stood stock still on the pavement outside.

Angus stood facing the shop window and looked at the multitude of jars containing any type of old-fashioned sweet you could imagine. He considered his reflection again and adjusted his jeans so they sat just right over his trainers. He ruffled up his damp gelled hair and then to his reflection he asked,

"Will it be the usual for you then?"

No reply came but he had seen a slight movement reflected in the glass and at that he stepped to the door. The bell jangled as he entered.

"Good morning Angus!" greeted Mrs James, "How's my best customer this morning?" she said, smiling broadly and folding her arms across her buttoned up cardigan.

"Hi Mrs James," he felt in his pocket for his money, "fine thanks."

"Now let me guess… cough candy is it?"

"Yes please… and a packet of mints as well thanks."
Angus stood for a moment outside the shop, just beside the
children's ride that had stood on the pavement for as long
as anyone could recollect and opened the small white
paper bag that contained the cough candy. He took one out
but instead of placing it in his mouth he looked around to
check that Mrs James was not watching and held it down to
his side.

"Fank ou," said a voice beside him.

"You're welcome… Meet you at the trees then?" asked
Angus glancing along the empty street.

"Mmmm… es… sorry yes," replied the muted voice.
If anyone had been watching they would think that Angus
was mad, what with talking to himself and feeding candy to
a children's ride. He turned away and popping a mint into
his own mouth, set off down the road grinning. He hunched
his shoulders a little more and braced himself against the
chill air. As he did this he recalled another time when he
had felt this cold. It was on a visit to Scotland. Pyrra had
flown there using her powers to slow time down and allow
them to travel vast distances in very little time at all. This
meant that Angus would not be missed and was a neat trick

the pair had used several times. There they had met Nathair the wyrm, an extremely unpleasant chap who got himself trapped in Loch Ness, only to be rescued by Angus. The memory of hitting the freezing water sent a chill running down Angus' spine. He had plunged into the murky depths from Pyrra's back and almost drowned as the icy water engulfed him. In the end Angus was okay and the secret of Loch Ness and its mysterious inhabitant was protected, but it was an experience he did not want to repeat in a hurry.

Angus finally reached the end of the High Street, turned left and headed for a small clump of trees. He weaved his way to the centre of the tiny wooded area, which had a clearing in the middle and took out another cough candy. As he did so, he felt warmth on his chest from the pouch he always had tied around his neck. Angus heard the soft crackle of frozen grass being trodden and felt an icy blast of wind rushing at him as Pyrra touched down lightly beside him.

"What kept you?" teased Angus.

"Well I was just about to follow you but a little girl came up with her mother just as you left. I couldn't morph until she had finished her ride and I didn't want to miss hearing

her young squeals of laughter… I hope that is for me,"
added Pyrra, eyeing the cough candy greedily.

"I thought you might be ready for another one by now,"
smiled Angus.
He held up the sweet and with the delicate grace of a
ballerina Pyrra picked it up between the fingers on one of
her fore claws so gently that Angus barely felt it. He
watched her as she placed the orange coloured confection
in her mouth and closed her eyes, savouring the aniseed
taste she loved so much.

Pyrra was a dragon and Angus was her protector. The
secret he kept so well was not only Pyrra's very existence
but that other dragons existed as well. Angus knew some of
them but he was also part of a society. The Secret Society
of Dragon Protectors to be exact, more commonly known
amongst its members as the SSDP. When he stopped to
think, it was amazing how it had all come about. Dragons
had always fascinated Angus and at the end of the school
year he discovered a book in the library that changed his
life forever. The book was 'Dragonalia' and he had learned
all he could about dragons from its pages. He had
befriended Miss Puttick, the local librarian in his home
town, and seeing his keenness for dragons she gave him a

pamphlet she had found hidden within its pages. The pamphlet had described to Angus a world of dragons in hiding and of a secret society sworn to protect them. The head of the society was Finian Tek and Angus wrote to him as requested in the pamphlet. Whilst waiting for an answer he had a chance to go to Piggleston with his parents, so Angus went in search of the dragon in the High Street, which he knew about from a much loved childhood story 'The Dragon's Tale'. Angus had not truly believed it was possible and when he came to the village in search of the storybook dragon, he was so stunned at what he found that his first reaction was to run away. However his curiosity got the better of him and he returned. Angus awoke Pyrra from her hiding place in the children's ride where the green dragon was seeing out the Great Hibernation. That was the name the dragons had given their self induced slumber, having decided to hide from mankind until it was safer for them to emerge and live freely once more. Only a chosen few humans knew the truth and they were sworn to protect the sleeping dragons. Soon Angus became a trusted friend of Pyrra and she confided in him about the other dragons she had once known. As to their whereabouts, she had no clue but, determined to help her find them, Angus set out to track down what he thought to be the original headquarters of the SSDP and with the help of Pyrra using dragon time they arrived at the Island of Calmor. Once there, Angus discovered that the SSDP did not have any active members left. Finian Tek, the last protector, died before passing on the responsibility to someone else. However Angus did discover some wall paintings of dragons in Calmor castle and with the help of Miss Puttick he was able to unlock the key to the hidden dragons. Together, Angus and Pyrra spent a fantastic summer holiday in each other's company, tracking down and re-awakening several of her dragon friends from their self-imposed hibernation, hidden away in everyday objects such as Pyrra had done with the children's ride.

"How have you been, Pyrra? Surely there's not that many children around in this weather to keep you busy!"

"No, not many… I expect they're all sensibly wrapped up indoors… how are things with you?" Angus' voice was on the verge of breaking and had an embarrassing habit of going up and down and all over the place at any moment in a sentence. Pyrra thought it was funny but was far too polite to say anything. After all, her voice had always been a bit creaky, but then she was nearly three thousand years old!

"Oh I'm great Pyrra… eh… any chance of a flight today?" he enquired hopefully.

"I thought you would never ask," she replied with a wry smile and a wink.

"Are you sure? It's just you look a little tired."

"Oh don't you worry about me. I'm fine… just not sleeping very well lately…" she replied hesitantly, but making a big effort she visibly brightened, "So! Where shall we go then?"

Angus considered his friend for a second before answering. He knew she was not being altogether truthful with him but he also realised she did not want to discuss it either, at least not just now.

"Anywhere Pyrra, you know it doesn't matter to me as long as you fly fast!" he replied with his usual enthusiasm. He pulled his hood a little tighter and jumped up onto her back. No sooner was he seated than Pyrra sprang from the ground using a massively powerful flap of her great wings. They seemed to take-off vertically from the ground like a rocket and Angus could not help yelling "WOOHOO!" at the top of his voice.

As they started to level out Angus relaxed his grip a little but still stayed in a low position, lying forward over Pyrra's back. He was not worried about making a noise or the risk of anyone seeing them because, as all protectors knew, you needed Dragonore to allow you to see through a dragon's disguise when they were invisible. It also enabled a dragon to recognise you as a protector and since all dragons had a piece of Dragonore on their chest it also allowed the dragons and protectors to sense when another dragon was near. This was very useful when trying to find new dragons. Which is something Angus had been helping Rathlin with over the last six months.

Calmor was now a secret dragon sanctuary and hive of activity with reawakened dragons visiting on a regular basis. Sometimes they went with protectors but mostly they went alone to meet up with old friends that had also been awakened from hibernation. With the comfort of the cavern under Calmor Castle they could freely roam around the island knowing that they were safe from humanity. Rathlin Tek had worked hard to mend the damage he had caused to the name of the society and with the help of Miss Puttick he had quite literally put his house in order. In fact Angus had noticed that she was spending a lot more time at Calmor recently.

He often visited the library to keep in touch with Miss Puttick, his great dragon ally and also unofficial guardian, as she usually kept an eye on him. His parents were still frantically tearing about the Home Counties in their green van, trying to save the world the 'Kleanware' way. They were always so busy running their all-consuming business, selling cleaning products from their converted garage that they never noticed if Angus was there or not half the time. It was not that they did not love him. Or that they did not care for him. They were just, well, busy. Always busy. Still he did not take advantage of their lack of interest in him and he went to school and did his homework. Angus was now in Year 7 at Kynton Comprehensive and Art was still the only lesson he really enjoyed. Naturally one of his favourite subjects to draw was dragons and his art teacher was amazed not only by his obvious talent but by his attention to detail. Of course Mr Neish had no idea that Angus actually knew several dragons personally and was drawing, as it were, from real life and not from his imagination at all!

Angus shook himself from his daydream as he realised that apart from missing the fun of flying with Pyrra, they were now taking a familiar route.

"Where are we going today Pyrra?" asked Angus already knowing the answer.

"Well I thought we could maybe visit Marnham," replied Pyrra quietly.

"Oh yeah... I thought we might be going there," he smiled.

"I just felt... well I... needed to have a chat with the boys," she justified.

Angus could sense Pyrra's unease, something troubled her and he was sensitive enough to her moods to know that something was wrong and she was not letting on.

"Pyrra... are you sure you're okay?" Angus probed gently.

"Yes I'm fine... it's just that... like I said, I'm not sleeping very well at the moment!"

"Why not? What's bothering you? Come on spill the beans."

"Look... I... no, it's nothing..."

"Pyrra... no more cough candies till you tell me," he teased.

"Well it sounds so silly... it's just that I've been having this dream and it keeps coming back night after night!" she turned her head round to face him, "There, I told you it was silly... it's nothing... just forget I told you."

"But what is this dream about?" Angus coaxed, feeling in his pocket for another cough candy.

"It's a dream about another dragon..."

"A dragon... really... which one... Godroi... Argent?" queried Angus insistently, his curiosity getting the better of him.

"No, no... none of the dragons I know. All I can tell you is that he is talking to me... It seems quite urgent because he's quite persistent and serious but I can't hear what he is saying."

"Wow Pyrra that's weird... but why is it so bad?"

"Well it's the same dream over and over again, every night."

"How long has that been happening?"

"A few days now..." she replied, "but it's strange because we dragons don't usually dream."

"What? Never!" exclaimed Angus, "You've never had a dream?"

"At least not until now… I can only assume that is what it was… I just wish I could make out what he is trying to tell me. It seems to be very important."

Pyrra turned to face Angus as she said that, and he could not help feeling sorry for her. She was his best friend and she was obviously distressed about the dream.

"Come on Pyrra, don't get upset… once you talk to the boys you'll feel better and maybe they will have an idea as to what all this is about."

"Yes, Godroi and Argent may be able to help… it's worth a try… thank you Angus… I really don't know why I was ashamed to tell you… that would be best. Then I can forget all about it and at least their antics will cheer me up." She increased the steady beating of her wings as if trying to raise her spirits by this action and headed southwest to the village of Marnham.

## Chapter 2

# *'Fascination with Gravel'*

It was thanks to both Angus and Miss Puttick that Pyrra was back in touch with her old friends Godroi and Argent. Godroi hibernated in a stained glass window depicting George and the Dragon. Argent, being a music lover, had morphed into a gargoyle on the same church roof, perfectly positioned to hear the organ music. Over the centuries both had been competing for Pyrra's affection and the three happily renewed their old companionship and friendly rivalry. The two dragons now had a protector and he was Hugh Penfold, the Vicar of St George's church in Marnham, and it was his church they lived on.

It was not long before Angus could see the familiar and very distinctive sight of the church in the distance as it had both a spire and a tower. Alighting in the churchyard and thoroughly chilled from the flight, Angus rubbed his cold hands together vigorously before blowing on them and putting them in his pockets. Pyrra had already made her way over to the church, as she was eager to discuss her dream with her friends. Argent was already down on the ground from his gargoyle perch waiting for them.

"Pyrra how wonderful to see you... I was hoping you would come today and lo and behold I sense the presence of your beauty approach," pronounced the silver-tongued Argent in his most flattering tone.

"Oh Argent you do talk such nonsense at times," she replied with a wry smile, "it's the Dragonore you sense and you know it."

Argent laughed out loud at being so transparent to Pyrra and turned to greet Angus instead.

"My goodness Angus you are getting taller and more handsome! We shall have to watch you with the ladies, won't we?" he teased.

"Hi Argent... I don't think so," replied Angus shyly.

"Where's Godroi? I have something important to tell you both," said Pyrra urgently.

"GODROI!" roared Argent. "He will no doubt be sleeping my dear... but we have something important to discuss with you also."

"What's this racket? Can't a simple dragon get a little peace without someone interrupting?" bellowed Godroi as he morphed out from his stained-glass window. He spotted Pyrra and immediately changed his mood. "Ah dear lady...

my apologies… had I known it was you I would have been here to greet you as you landed."

"You mean you didn't sense her!" teased Argent with feigned surprise and pleased to gain the upper hand with his old rival.

"Now boys, let's not start… I'm here to discuss something very important with you both," she said, keen to focus on the problem.

Angus could see that the antics of Godroi and Argent had in fact cheered Pyrra up already. He loved to accompany her on her visits to 'the boys' as she liked to call them. They always put on a show for her, trying to win her approval by verbally jousting with each other. He would watch as they played off one another like some comedy double act and could see how happy they would be when it made Pyrra smile. However this time Pyrra had something too important to tell them. Godroi looked at her very closely as if considering something.

"My dear… so sorry… I can see you are not quite yourself today… come, tell us what is bothering you," he said.

"Yes please do. If a lady in distress needs help, then we are the very dragons for the job," added Argent quite unnecessarily.

Just then a rather short, plump man wearing a long white cassock walked around the corner from the front end of the church. Angus thought the man's appearance was funny because he wore a purple woolly hat with a bobble on his head and a yellow scarf wrapped tightly around his clerical dog collar. The scarf trailed down over his cassock and he kept hitching them both up to make sure he did not trip over. However he was not very successful and stumbled his way along the uneven path. All this, combined with his chubby face and rosy cheeks, made him seem quite comical as he shuffled into sight.

Suddenly Angus caught sight of a girl about his own age behind the man. Being just twelve, Angus had not really taken much notice of girls before. They never bothered with him at school as he was not sporty, nor did he tease them like the other boys in his class did. This girl however took his breath away! She had long chestnut hair swept up with a clip and neatly hanging down at the back with her fringe framing her face. She had pretty eyes, a small nose and a friendly smile. Angus felt his stomach churning as he hung back trying not to stare but he really wanted to know who this girl was.

"Ah Godroi... Argent... there you are... I wondered where you had got to. I was just looking for you inside as I had something I wanted you to see. Remember we spoke about it?" said the jolly Vicar in a sing song voice.

"Ah Hugh... yes of course, my apologies... something else came up and I think you may want to hear it as well," replied Godroi knowingly as he looked at Pyrra. As if sensing her unease at the new faces he continued, "Firstly let me introduce everyone, Pyrra... this is Hugh Penfold, the gentleman who now kindly looks after us and allows us to remain in his wonderful church."

"Delighted to meet you Pyrra," said the Vicar as he bowed slightly in her direction, the oversized bobble on his hat flopping ridiculously. "I've heard so much about you from Argent and Godroi that I feel I know you already."

"Really!" she replied glancing at the other dragons, "I do hope it was all good... and I am honoured to meet you sir."

"Ahem... er... yes... and this is his lovely daughter Georgina," added Godroi hastily.

"I am very honoured to meet you too," added Pyrra extending a claw to shake hands, "It's nice to see that we have some more girls in the ranks at last."

"Oh I'm not a protector…" she blushed, glancing in the direction of Angus, "although someday I would love to be one."

"And who is this fine fellow hiding in the background?" asked the Vicar indicating Angus who was still awestruck by the girl.

"Ah this is our saviour!" boomed Godroi, "Without Angus we would still all be sleeping away in hibernation with who knows what happening to us."

"Angus!" exclaimed the Vicar taking his hand, "My word you are an honoured visitor…" he continued shaking Angus,' hand so much that the lad felt himself almost being lifted off the stone path. "Please excuse my attire but I was in church this morning and threw on the first hat and scarf I could find to come outside… Georgina this is Angus do you recall the stories we were told about him… quite the hero by all accounts."

By this time Angus was bright red with embarrassment and with Georgina looking so closely at him he was wishing the ground would just open up and swallow him whole. He would rather face an evil monster than be here right now.

"Hi!" replied Angus shyly to Georgina, while at the same time trying not to look directly at her. The Vicar finally released Angus' hand from his hearty grasp and the boy risked a quick glance at Georgina again. She grinned at him oblivious to his discomfort. He blushed even more and returned the smile weakly before turning back to her father. "I couldn't have done it without Pyrra..." he mumbled.

"So modest as well... you shall have to come here for tea someday and tell us all about your heroics first hand, I'm sure Georgina would like that... wouldn't you dear?" he said turning to his daughter.

"Yes I would Daddy," she replied looking at Angus, acutely aware of his discomfort.

"Now what is it you want me to hear?" asked Hugh. Pyrra straight away launched into an account of her disturbing dream, unburdening her troubles on her trusted male dragon friends. Godroi and Argent stood rooted to the spot, listening to every word and then Argent spoke slowly in hushed tones, without his usual joviality.

"We have both been having the same dream… Godroi and I, and it must be something important if you are having it as well… although we don't know what it means either".

"The dream seems to be about an old dragon deep in a cave with a large glowing wall of some kind behind him," added Godroi.

"Don't any of you recognise the place?" asked Angus forgetting his shyness with the girl for the moment and reverting to his usual inquisitive self.

"I'm afraid not Angus," replied Godroi.

"It's a bit of a mystery," added Argent.

"I felt he was trying to tell us something important but I can't make out the words. I wonder if any other dragons are having the same dream?" finished Pyrra.

"I think I will have to call Rathlin and Miss Puttick… maybe they will know what to do or even have something like this mentioned in the Tower Room at Calmor" suggested Angus.

"That is a good idea Angus" nodded the Vicar approvingly, "Ever the man of action."

Angus realised everyone including Georgina now looked at him and he suddenly became very self-conscious again. He blushed and dropped his gaze to look at the suddenly fascinating gravel path he stood on. The six figures stood on the path in Marnham churchyard and made-up the strangest group you could ever imagine. Each one silently pondered the possible meaning of the dream that had disturbed all three dragons.

## Chapter 3

# 'Return to Calmor'

Godroi was first to break the silence

"Well now… I believe you have something important to do as well," he said looking at the Vicar, tactfully diverting the attention from the still bright-red Angus.

"Ah yes of course Godroi, thank you for reminding me." Hugh Penfold reached into the deep pocket of his cassock and held out his hand towards his daughter. Georgina now gave her full attention to her father and Angus watched her quizzical expression turn to delight as her father pinned a tiny intricate brooch in the shape of a dragon, on her jacket. "The eye is a piece of Dragonore," the vicar explained to everyone. He obviously enjoyed her pleasure at his gift as she handled it and turned it to her smiling face. "I thought I should give you something to mark your acceptance into the Society" he smiled, "You will officially be Godroi's protector now."

The golden dragon beamed at Georgina and she at him.

They were of course already friends and it made sense to have someone trustworthy as a protector. Now with her father as Argent's protector they could keep an eye on the two church dragons together and Angus knew he would have another chance to meet Georgina, a thought that pleased and also terrified him. Just as the dragons were adding their support and congratulations, Georgina looked over at Angus and caught him staring at her. In his embarrassment at being caught Angus once again looked down at his feet and studied his trainers very intensely. She was not sure if Angus was just shy or being rude and with a toss of her clipped up hair she turned away from him. She linked arms with her father and they walked back to the old church, having said their goodbyes to the dragons. Angus was now very anxious to end his discomfort and to be off.

"Pyrra we have things to do… we had better go," he said.

Pyrra said her goodbyes to the other two dragons and soon took off with Angus on her back.

On the way home from Marnham, with the weak winter sun still attempting to break through the heavy clouds gathering overheard, Angus had another idea.

"Pyrra, why don't we check on Rhys and see if she is having the dream?" he suggested.

"That's a good idea Angus... you seem very keen to discover what's happening," she replied.

"I am... this is all too weird... three of you having the same dream over and over. There has to be a reason and I want to find out what it is, don't you?" he asked.

"Of course I do... I'm just a bit scared of what it might mean."

"YOU... scared! No way Pyrra... whatever it is, we can sort it out... no problem."
The dragon did not reply as she still pondered her own thoughts about the stranger in the dream and what message he seemed so intent on telling them.

Soon they flew into a bare garden, glistening with frost and Angus recognised the dragon-shaped weather vane on top of the house. They found Rhys morphed in her usual statue guise, but the garden, which held so much beauty and scent in the summer, looked rather dreary and almost dead in February. Angus stood with his mouth open as the gorgeous red dragon appeared in all her splendour in front of him.

"Angus how lovely to see you again!" she purred.

"Hi Rhys… nice to see you as well" he replied softly. Unlike the other dragons Rhys was very feminine looking as far as dragons went and she was also a great subject to draw. Angus wished he had brought the drawing of Rhys he had done during a recent art mock exam. The teacher had set them the task of drawing a vase of flowers, which Angus had done well enough. However as he always did, he had managed to place a dragon into the picture. 'It was his signature' his teacher had explained at parents evening to his baffled Mum and Dad. So because he was drawing flowers he had immediately thought of Rhys in her garden and had placed her in the picture as if smelling the beautiful fragrance of the flowers that her garden provided during the summer. As much as Angus admired other dragons, one was irreplaceable in his eyes and he tuned back into Pyrra as she told Rhys what had brought them to the garden in such bitter weather.

"Have you been dreaming at all?" Pyrra enquired, getting straight to the point.

At first Rhys did not say a word, she just glared at Pyrra.

"Why should you ask such a question? You know we don't dream."

Rhys seemed reluctant to answer and she avoided eye contact with Pyrra as the green dragon continued to probe.

"Look Rhys I know we have not always seen eye to eye but trust me, this is important…" Pyrra paused, dropped her head with a sigh and continued while staring at the ground, "You see… I have been having these… strange dreams" she looked up at Rhys, "and so have the boys."
Rhys just stared at the green dragon in total shock. Now Pyrra had the red dragon's full attention she might get a proper answer. As far as Angus was aware, they were friends but from the way they acted together he could see things had not always been good between them. Pyrra knew she had to keep trying, as she was sure Rhys was having the dream. Bringing herself up to her full height she tried again.

"The dream contains an old dragon in a large cavern… the wall behind is glowing and he seems to be saying something…"

"I should say! Some old dragon telling me to… 'Aweccan, gemunan', and something else…" she blurted out, interrupting Pyrra, "but I have no idea what it means or why I am even having visions in the night!"

"Well we've all been having the same dream, you, me and the boys," replied Pyrra casting a knowing smile to Angus.

"But we do not dream!" said an obviously flustered but relieved Rhys, "It's all very disturbing and I can't get a decent nights sleep."

"I know it's very frustrating… for all of us," confirmed Pyrra.

"The thing is Rhys, no-one knows where he is… did you recognise the place at all?" joined in Angus.

"No I don't… and I have never seen that dragon before."

"Well at least we know you are all in the same boat," replied Angus, "and now we know some of what he is saying… thanks to you."

Rhys was pleased to have been some use and once they had said farewell, Angus and Pyrra set off having promised Rhys that they would try to get to the bottom of the dream.

The flight home was short as Pyrra had gone into dragon time as soon as they were airborne. Angus was glad of this as it gave him time to think about the message and he looked down on things below that appeared to be almost frozen in time. Cars looked stationary on the roads, three riders galloped on their horses but got nowhere; and a high speed train that seemed to be crawling at a snail's pace were just some of the things he spotted. None of this helped relax him though, as his mind buzzed, trying to work out why his friends were all having the same strange dream. As soon as he got home Angus dialled Rathlin's number and was not really surprised when Miss Puttick answered the phone.

"Hi Miss P, it's Angus," he replied to her librarian's posh phone voice.

"Oh Angus you must be telepathic, Rathlin and I were just talking about you" she enthused down the phone. "We have something to tell y…"

"Sorry Miss P but I have something really important to tell you! Something weird has happened and I need your help," interrupted Angus.

"Of course Angus, whatever is the matter dear… please tell me?" she asked, now with more than a hint of concern in her voice.

"It's Pyrra. She is having a dream of some sort and when we visited Godroi and Argent, they are having it as well…"

"Oh my… I think I know what you are talking about…"

"You do?"

"Cyru has been having dreams about an old dragon trying to say something to him, but he can't make out what," finished Miss Puttick.

"Yeah I know, Pyrra and the boys couldn't either but we just came back from seeing Rhys and she told us the first two words," revealed Angus.

"Marvellous Angus... what are they?" she asked eagerly.

"'Aweccan, gemunan'... she couldn't make out the rest," he confirmed.

"Well this certainly is an astonishing phenomenon Angus. We know dragons do not dream and we thought it was only Cyru having this experience, but now... well I think I need to discuss this with Rathlin... can I call you back?"

"Yeah no problem, I have some homework I can do for a while... listen I was hoping that Rathlin might have the answer amongst all that stuff that Finian left in the Tower Room," he said hopefully.

"You may be correct Angus but I am still trying to catalogue and index it. That room is in such a mess, I think

I have only just touched the tip of the iceberg as they say," she replied.

"Oh… okay… well please don't take too long to call me back… I really want to find out what's going on… Pyrra is quite upset by these dreams."

"Cyru is too and it's no wonder… don't worry I won't be long… bye Angus."

Angus replaced the handset in its holder and tried to collect his thoughts. The morning had started out so simply. All he had in mind was a chat with Pyrra and a fast and furious flight into the clouds and back, but now everything was upset by this dream.

Angus stepped out into the chill afternoon. Already it had begun to get dark and he decided it would be best to send Pyrra back home to Piggleston. He found her at the side of the garage trying to stay warm against the building. It was just as well she was invisible. If his Mum and Dad could see a fully-grown green dragon lying at the side of the house, 'they would absolutely freak out big time' he thought with a smirk.

"Hello Angus… well what did Rathlin have to say then?" she asked anxiously.

"It was Miss Puttick that answered and she told me that Cyru is having the same dream as well."

"Cyru too… it must be affecting us all then," she nodded, "did she say anything else?"

"Not really… they thought it was only Cyru but when I told her about the words Rhys recalled from the dream she went to speak to Rathlin and said she would call back shortly," answered Angus.

Pyrra did not look happy but she could see Angus' concern and made an attempt at feigned cheerfulness.

"Well at least something is happening… maybe I could stay here for a while just in case anything turns up."

"Well I have some homework to do and I need to be inside so I can hear the phone… don't you think you would be better off in Piggleston?" suggested Angus.

"You are probably right Angus but I would prefer to hear what is going to happen first… but you go and do your homework please. I will be fine just here," she replied obstinately, "However, I will have one of those sweets I can smell in your pocket."

Angus knew there would be no arguing with her in this mood.

"Okay if you're sure…" he laughed fishing out the cough candy, "Here you go" he said as he tossed one up to Pyrra.

Angus had been trying to do his homework for about twenty-five minutes now. Well twenty-six minutes and ten seconds to be exact. He had read question four of his maths homework at least three times and it still had not sunk in yet. It was now dark outside and he was getting impatient. All he wanted to do was find out why all the dragons were having these dreams and somehow put a stop to the distress it was causing. He had checked on Pyrra once more and she seemed to be dozing. Although he had a doubt as to how deep a sleep she would be in. The dream seemed to disturb her, as it did all the dragons. He read the question again in a fit of concentration. $8(y+3) = 4(y+8)$ Ah, now he understood it. He started to scribble the answer down and managed to get through the next two equations without looking at the clock again. Just as he realised it was nearly dinnertime that he heard the high pitched ring of the phone. He vaulted down the stairs and grabbed the phone just as his Mum got there.

"I've got it!" he shouted as he dived for the handset and grabbed it from the holder.

"Angus..." shouted his Mum, "please don't jump down the stairs like that!" she chided.

"Sorry Mum," he replied sheepishly.
She turned back towards the kitchen and shouted over her shoulder that dinner would be ready soon and not to be too long, but Angus was already pressing the green button to answer the call.

"Hi, Angus speaking, can I help you," he stated, just as he had been taught.

"Angus it's me, Rathlin. How are you lad?"

"I'm fine Rathlin, how are things? Did you manage to discover anything?" whispered Angus urgently.

"I'm afraid we haven't yet but we're still looking... listen we could do with some help and Aurora and I also have something else to tell you... nothing serious mind, just some personal news we have... can you come here to Calmor soon?" he barely managed before Angus answered.

"I could come tomorrow and I'm sure Pyrra will welcome the diversion," Angus butted in.
He finished the call and on the pretence of emptying the bin he went out to the garage to tell Pyrra the plan. Angus was happy to see that the news had perked her up and both

were extremely pleased to be doing something positive. Angus returned to the house after Pyrra flew off into the night sky. They had decided to meet first thing in the morning.

At the dinner table Angus played with his food wondering what news Miss P and Rathlin had for him.

"What's the matter dear?" asked his Mum.

"Eh… oh nothing… just not hungry Mum," he replied lacking his usual spark.

"I wouldn't be surprised if you are coming down with something what with all that running about you do outside," she said.

"I'm fine Mum honest… just tired that's all," fibbed Angus.

"Well your Dad and I are going out for a bit… will you be okay?" she asked as his Dad glanced up from the orders he was checking at the kitchen table.

"Yeah… I'll be fine… I've got homework and I want to get an early night anyway," he replied.

"Good lad," said his Dad to the papers on the table. Angus helped clear the table and gave his self absorbed parents a kiss goodbye as they left before going upstairs to finish off his homework. He went to bed early as he had told his parents and tried to get a good night's sleep before the long flight to Calmor.

Early next morning Angus placed his bike against the railings at the small park and chained it up as he always did. He felt tired from what turned out to have been a very restless night. He was sure that it was just his own imagination but for a split second or two he could see the old dragon. The same one the others had described but it was silly because he was human and it surely only affected the dragons. It was probably just because they had spoken about it all day yesterday and his mind was playing tricks. He certainly did not see the dragon talk as it was never in his dream long enough, but it returned several times during the night. Angus put it out of his mind just as Pyrra landed on the wet grass.

Wordlessly Angus jumped up with his backpack and pulled his heavy jacket's zipper further up to cover his face. Pyrra sprang into the air and began to beat her wings until they rose silently up and into the dark, ominous looking clouds. It was not long before Pyrra switched to dragon time. This was the name that Angus had given the ability all dragons had to magically alter time. They could slow time down for themselves, thus allowing the outside world to fly past while they aged very slowly. This was what they did when they hibernated. They could also speed time up for themselves, allowing them to travel great distances in what seemed like minutes or a couple of hours. Distances that would take others a lot longer to traverse by conventional means.

As Pyrra settled into her usual steady rhythm Angus had time to recall some of the events of last summer and his previous visit to Calmor Castle. In fact it had been a blur of action jumping from one part of the country to another; locating Pyrra's lost friends. Then they found out about the sinister man in black who was also looking for dragons. Little could they have imagined that he was none other than the brother of Finian Tek or that he was using the knowledge he had gained by default to try and trap a dragon for his own amusement. This brother took it upon himself to try and scare Angus, thus giving himself away. That was when Angus, Pyrra and Miss Puttick decided to take matters into their own hands. They all flew to Calmor and managed to find a hidden underground cavern that used to shelter the dragons long ago in an age when they were more able to move freely to and from Calmor. Unfortunately for the adventurers they were trapped and although Angus managed to escape he came face to face with Finian's brother, Rathlin, in a dramatic showdown. After finally listening to reason in the form of Miss Puttick and Angus, Rathlin made amends by re-establishing the SSDP the way Finian would have wanted and by recruiting Angus as the first official protector for many years. Angus had never wanted anything more in the world and he looked down at Pyrra's noble head as she flew steadily through the clouds, he was still just as determined to protect her from anything and everything he could. Now that he thought about it he was amazed that he had not been back to Calmor since their last eventful visit when they had confronted Rathlin. Since then he had helped Rathlin find and reawaken quite a few dragons. Angus had always met him somewhere along the way, Rathlin with Cyru and Angus as always accompanied by Pyrra.

After about two hours of flying, Angus knew that they should almost be there. In fact the first time they had flown to Calmor they had nearly collided with a glider and Angus was left hurtling towards ground before Pyrra had rescued him. Now they started to slowly descend to the Irish Sea and it was not long before the cloud cover had cleared enough for Angus to see their destination.

The sea was dark and angry looking. He could see the waves lashing the rocks around the little islands that made up The Maidens. He would be glad to get his feet on the ground and warm himself at the fireside in the Great Hall of Calmor. Suddenly Pyrra started to descend more rapidly and fly straight at the cliff face just below the castle. At first Angus was stunned and a little concerned but then he realised that they were heading for the concealed entrance that would take them to the great doors of the hidden cavern. Angus could see the coveted plant, Blue Dragon Fire, hanging over the entrance, its vibrant blue flowers shivering in the violent weather. Pyrra streamlined her wings and dived headlong for the opening causing Angus to instinctively duck. Just after they passed through the veil of green and blue Pyrra spread her great wings and gracefully touched down on the stone floor at the far side of the entrance. Angus could see at the jetty, a small boat bobbing up and down as far as the mooring ropes would allow. The large doors, with the strange dragon writings above, lay open and inviting with a multitude of fiery torches illuminating the cavern beyond. Miss Puttick and Rathlin stood in the doorway waiting to greet them as they landed.

"I hope the flight wasn't too wild?" said Rathlin, welcoming Angus with a steadying hand on his shoulder as soon as his feet had touched the stone floor.

"No it was fine. Pyrra is a great flyer," he replied honestly.

"It is so good to see you Angus," said Miss Puttick as she pulled him into a great hug, "My you are soaking wet... we need to get you upstairs to the fire... but first we have another development that both of you need to see... Pyrra how are you darling?" she finished, turning her attention to the dragon as Rathlin welcomed her.

"I am fine Aurora... just a little tired," replied Pyrra as they started to move into the corridor that led to the main cavern.

"I'm sure you are dear. With these dreams disturbing your sleep it must be very draining... hopefully we can find a way to stop them."

"I hope so," replied Pyrra.

"So what is it you want to show us?" asked Angus always impatient and inquisitive.

"We need you to meet someone… someone who is new to us but certainly not to Calmor," replied Rathlin.

"Can't you just tell us?" asked Angus eagerly.

"Now that would spoil the surprise Angus and that is no fun at all!" laughed Miss Puttick.

Angus shrugged his shoulders and as they walked he was pleased to see that the large cage Rathlin had previously used to keep Cyru in was no longer there. They were being led to the other side of the cavern, past the niches that lined the almost circular cavern wall, to a cave at the other side. It was strange that Angus had never noticed it before but then there had been a lot going on during his last visit. They went in and as there were no lit torches it took Angus' eyes a few seconds to adjust to the darkness. A hitherto unexplored cavern lay beyond the cave entrance and as they entered it seemed like another corridor. As they walked further Angus could see anterooms off either side, surely big enough for a dragon to rest in. At the farthest end of the cave in the darkest corner was an even deeper and more foreboding cave.

"Are we going in there?" asked Angus warily.

"No, in here!" replied Pyrra looking into a dimly lit hollow which was off to one side.

Angus peered past Pyrra and squinted trying to focus his eyes on the recumbent figure beyond. He could see Cyru and was about to greet him when he spotted another smaller dragon lying behind the blue dragon. Cyru was leaning in close, deep in conversation with an ancient stranger the likes of which Angus had never seen before.

"This is what we wanted you to see. His name is Hereward," explained Miss Puttick.

"You said he wasn't new to Calmor, but I'm sure he wasn't here before. Where did you find him?" asked Angus who did not miss a trick.

"That's the thing Angus... he has always been here," explained Rathlin, "Hereward was hibernating in Calmor all the time... Finian apparently found him many years ago and led him here..." he turned to the old dragon, "ever since then he was

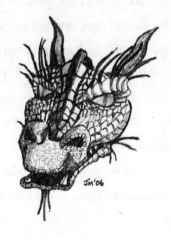

back in deep hibernation."

"You mean he was here all the time?" asked an incredulous Angus.

"Yes and it seems that when Finian found Hereward he was in danger of being discovered. He was getting far too old and was blind so Finian brought him here... at least that's what Hereward has explained so far... but we can't find a thing in Finian's records about him," explained Miss Puttick.

Pyrra had already gone in to speak to Hereward and was obviously speaking in dragon so no doubt she would be getting the same story. Angus studied the old dragon, his eyes were glassy and unseeing, his face covered with whiskers. His dark greyish scales were starting to peel and he looked very ancient indeed, certainly a different generation to Pyrra and her friends.

"Who's that with you?" Hereward may have been old and blind but his hearing was extremely acute.

"This is Angus," said Pyrra, "He's the one Cyru told you about."

"Ah Angus... yes... you are the one that found Pyrra and saved Cyru..." he said to the floor with his right ear facing Angus, "it's a pity dear Finian could not have met you."

"How long have you been here?" Angus asked.

"Well it's hard to tell… I have been sleeping since Finian brought me here, but I think he was a young man when I met him" explained Hereward in his soft and ancient tones.

"From what we can gather he has been in this cave for at least twenty years" added Rathlin.

"Wow… so how did you find Hereward?" asked Angus eagerly.

"He found us! Well… Cyru to be exact after the dream woke him up last night" finished Miss Puttick.

"So you've had the dream too?' cried Angus in his eagerness.

"Yes young man… never happened before" continued Hereward, "strange thing though… the messenger is a very ancient dragon… too old to still be alive."

"How old?" asked Angus.

"Well I am nearly four thousand years old, a few years more than these youngsters here… he would be far older than that… maybe more than six thousand years old" he replied sagely.

"Six thousand years old!" shouted Angus "No way!"

"Yes way, young man… I just told you so didn't I?" replied the old dragon rather testily, not understanding that Angus did actually believe him and leaving the others suppressing sniggers, "I feel I know where he is… that strange light blue glow is familiar but alas I cannot quite recollect…"

"Did you hear the words?" probed Angus eagerly.

"Yes, yes I did… 'Aweccan, gemunan ac gecierran'," replied Hereward

"If only we knew what it meant," added Miss Puttick.

"'Reawaken, remember and return'," translated Hereward, "it's Old English."

"Of course it is!" confirmed Miss Puttick.

"Did he say anything else to you Hereward?" asked Pyrra.

"No, he just kept telling me to 'Reawaken, remember and return'… if only I knew where old Barfoot was to be found."

"You just said Barfoot… who's that?" asked Angus.

"Did I… really…Barfoot… yes that was his name… could not recall it before… seems to have just come out," smiled Hereward toothlessly.

Having discussed the old dragon's interpretation of the dream it was not long before they had persuaded him to go outside for some fresh air. They led Hereward through the caves, up the secret passage to the cellar and into the Great Hall. It was mid morning now and when they opened the large Celtic emblazoned doors they were surprised to see that the wind had died a little and the sun was attempting to shine. They escorted the oldest living dragon they knew and settled him in a patch of Blue Dragon Fire. All dragons dearly loved the plant as its aniseed aroma gave them a sense of well-being and happiness. Leaving him reminiscing with Pyrra and Cyru, Rathlin, Miss Puttick and Angus went back inside the castle wondering who the mysterious Barfoot was and why the dragons were dreaming about him.

## Chapter 4

# 'The Cor Stan'

The human contingent stopped and warmed themselves at the roaring fire in the Great Hall before they made their way to the Turret Room that had served as a storeroom for all the information on dragons that Finian had collated over the years. 'At last' thought Angus! He had been dying to enter the inner sanctum of the revived SSDP. In fact, by the look of the volumes of stuff that greeted them, some of it was collected by Tek ancestors as well. There were piles of parchments; stacks upon stacks of books; drawings of dragons; note books with hand-written scribbles and sketches; and all sorts of objects ranging from boxes to replicas of bones. It was a complete mess and Angus laughed when he spotted the look on Miss Puttick's face.

"That is not helping me one bit Angus, you know how I hate disorder," she scolded with a hint of a smile.

"I thought you were going to sort this lot out?" teased Angus.

"I have started it as you can see from the piles but someone keeps moving things around," she said as she glared at Rathlin.

"I have not touched a thing Aurora," he replied holding up his hands in contrition. "Anyway what are we looking for?" he asked changing the subject.
She smiled at his attempt to look all innocent.

"Well I think we should start by looking for the name Barfoot... that's our best bet," replied Miss Puttick, "Angus you start there and Rathlin you over here," she had directed Angus to a large pile of papers on the top of a filing cabinet. He watched Miss Puttick and Rathlin and it really amazed him they had become such good friends. She was a prim librarian and Rathlin was the surly master of Calmor. It was only six months ago that she had slapped him hard on the face after he had trapped them in the cavern below. He was the owner of Calmor Castle and now, not only a good friend to both of them, but to all dragons as well. With Miss Puttick's help Rathlin tried to sort out the wealth of dragon protecting knowledge his brother Finian had left behind. The whole family estate, including all the dragon information, went to Rathlin when Finian died a few years ago. Rathlin had been estranged from his brother for many years and his bitterness had made him not only a bully, but his enforced exclusion from the dragons had warped his understanding of the Society and its aims. He wanted to collect dragons for all the wrong reasons and was now totally reformed and a different man altogether. He had revived the Secret Society of Dragon Protectors and was running it in the way his dead brother Finian would surely have approved.

As Angus looked around he could see that Miss Puttick had been busy trying to create order out of chaos and had been cataloguing Finian's discoveries with the precision of a librarian's orderly mind during her frequent visits to Calmor. As Angus thumbed through Finian's lists looking for a dragon of the name Barfoot, Dermot the warden entered the room and as usual, magically produced tea and flapjacks.

"Well now tis young Angus if am not mistaken," he smiled, "sure you're a sight for sore eyes" he said in his broad Irish accent.

"Hi Dermot good to see you… how are the dogs?" asked Angus with a cheeky grin.
Dermot lived in the lighthouse at the end of the island and assisted Rathlin with the running of the castle. He also

looked after the well-being of Rathlin's dogs. They were huge hunting hounds, the short coated wiry breed and Angus remembered his run in with them the last time they met, only just being saved from a mauling by Rathlin.

"Oh well now they would be fine," he laughed recognising the humour, "I'm keeping them locked up in a special run I built over at the lighthouse. That way they won't be bothering any of our other guests and they would still be getting plenty of exercise." he winked, "So you'll be wanting to come over an give them a clap then will ya?"

"Er... maybe later," replied Angus with a smile on his face.

Dermot laughed out loud and bade them goodbye leaving them to savour his flapjacks and drink the tea. It was while he munched on his third flapjack that Angus noticed Miss Puttick had been unusually quiet since coming to the Turret Room; obviously she had something on her mind. He watched her fidgeting with some paperwork she had already sorted through twice and it was clear her mind was not on the task at hand. She must have sensed him staring at her and looking up at him, broke her silence.

"Angus I have something important to tell you…"

Miss Puttick had been dying to tell Angus her news and now she seized her chance.

"Nothing's wrong I hope!" said Angus worried by her tone.

"No, no... It's just that... Rath has asked me to marry him and... well... of course I've said yes!" she squealed losing her usual composure. "The wedding will be here in Calmor at Easter and I want you and Pyrra to be there!" she finished into a stunned silence.

Angus was so shocked that he had to put his cup down quickly and in doing so knocked over the pile of papers he had been working through all over the floor.

"onrat... orry... congratulations!" he spluttered, spraying crumbs everywhere.

With Rathlin highly amused at his surprise Angus scrabbled to pick up the papers whist trying to speak at the same time.

"Thank you," smiled Rathlin and Miss Puttick together, "Oh don't bother with that just now" added Miss Puttick grabbing him for a quick and embarrassing hug.

While all this went on, Angus had spotted a particular paper entitled 'dragon hierarchy' that had caught his eye on the floor and he put it carefully on top of the filing cabinet to look at later. Miss Puttick demanded his full attention and went on about how it was all thanks to Angus that they had met in the first place.

"So you'll be moving up here and giving up the library?" asked Angus.

"Well yes… I am sad about that… but I will be carrying on a more noble cause with Rathlin," she answered, "and anyway he needs me here to keep him in line," she finished smiling up at Rathlin.

It all seemed a bit sudden, but given the age of these love-struck adults Angus supposed they knew what they were doing. They spent the next hour talking about wedding plans and the paper on top of the filing cabinet was quite forgotten. Soon it was time to go and having said goodbye the pair set course for home. It was almost dark and Angus told Pyrra about the wedding.

"That is wonderful," was her reply and she talked about it all the way home and how she had never been to a wedding before. Pyrra was excited about attending her first wedding but Angus wondered how he could persuade his parents to let him go to Calmor for a few days. Would they wonder about how he would get there? He would have to pretend he was travelling up with Miss P, rather than flying on a dragon's back. That was funny he'd have to start thinking of her as 'Mrs T 'soon!

The Munros were predictably un-phased by Angus' announcement over dinner that night as they were engrossed in the launch of a new range of ecological cleaning products.

"That's nice for her dear... " replied his Mum rather distractedly. Then as if the news had just sunk in. "Isn't she a bit old for that sort of thing?" she asked.

"Miss P seems to be happy Mum and she really wants me to go... Can I?" he implored with the most appealing face he could muster.

"Well if your Dad says its okay," she conceded.

"Eh... Wha...?" mumbled Angus' Dad as his concentration on the imminent launch of the new Kleanware product range was broken.

"Angus was asking if he could go." he still looked none the wiser, "to the wedding... oh Donald pay attention."

"Sorry love... okay when is this wedding?" he replied.

"Easter... and Angus would be away for a few days with Aurora Puttick," again the blank look, "you know, the librarian!" This was proving to be hard work.

"And who's getting married?" he asked with a completely confused and stupid look on his face.

"MISS PUTTICK!" replied Mrs Munro, raising her voice in an exasperated manner.

"Is she really? Well I never... Isn't she a bit old to be getting married?" he asked, smiling vacantly as he tried to catch up with the conversation.

Angus almost burst out laughing but just managed to keep his face straight. He found his parents' lack of interest in anything not connected to Kleanware somewhat infuriating, even if it was amusing at times.

"Obviously not... so can he go?" She finally got there.

"Eh... well... what do you think dear?"

"Oh for goodness sake!" she said to his Dad before turning to Angus and immediately softening her manner, "of course you can dear just make sure we get all the contact details... and I wouldn't mind a quick chat with Aurora before you go."

Angus was used to that type of conversation in the house as it always took his Dad a bit longer to catch up, on the rare occasion that he did. On the whole Angus got off lightly, the only other conditions Mum gave him was that his schoolwork had to be up to date and he had to help them with stuffing envelopes and delivering Kleanware products before he went off. That would have happened anyway, so Angus did not see that as an extra chore. They had not even asked him how he would get there, so the lie about the journey Angus had in reserve did not need to be told. He was delighted at the prospect of the Calmor wedding and the Easter holidays could not come soon enough! It was not so much the thought of the event itself, Miss P had told him that Hugh Penfold would be officiating at the ceremony and Angus privately hoped that the Vicar's daughter, Georgina, would be there as well.

Angus kept his promise to the other dragons and with Pyrra's help he visited them all during the week, reassuring them that they were not the only ones having dragon dreams. They still had to figure out what the message was all about, as well as who the mysterious Barfoot was and why they were all dreaming about him. He did not tell anyone that he was having the dream as well or that it was getting stronger every night.

The next week took an aeon to pass and Angus' frustration was increased after he sneaked off to visit Pyrra and found her still very much disturbed by the dream. His inability to do anything for her was confounded by the news from Miss Puttick that they were still none the wiser about the persistent Barfoot. In fact it was a thoroughly impatient Angus Munro who arrived back at Calmor the following weekend. Angus escaped his parents' Kleanware delivery tasks by pretending to be out for a bike ride and although they made good use of dragon time he was still aware that it had taken them a little longer than usual to get there, such was Pyrra's state.

"I'm going to go and find Rathlin or Miss P, will you be okay?" asked Angus watching Pyrra closely for signs of tiredness.

"I'll be fine now that I'm surrounded by Blue Dragon Fire," she replied smiling and certainly looked happier than she had been earlier.

Pyrra wandered off outside, free to roam in the Island sanctuary and looked for other dragons. Angus watched her for a few seconds as she walked away majestically stretching her wings before tucking them neatly along her body. Once he was satisfied that she was settled he entered the castle, running his hand over the vast wooden door with its Celtic symbols. Not for the first time did he marvel at the solidity of the wood and wonder what tales the great portal could tell. Miss Puttick came to the Hall to greet him, clucking away like an overexcited hen,

"Angus!" she shouted, "you're here… I've been so worried. I thought you would have been here sooner."

"Well we…" he tried to say.

She grabbed him into a rough hug snuffing out his words and shepherded him over to the big fireplace.

"You are chilled to the bone… sit down and have some hot cocoa… now then, what kept you?" she demanded, weighing him up concernedly.

"Give the lad a chance!" added Rathlin from the other couch giving Angus a sly wink, "He can hardly get a word in".

"Thanks… We just took a little longer than usual" replied Angus looking serious, "To be honest this dream is really tiring Pyrra and she is not feeling that great… though she won't admit it."

"I'm sure she will be fine," replied Rathlin, "she's strong, as are the rest and being here should revive her… it seems to help the others," he added.

They talked for a while, mostly about the wedding. At least Miss Puttick talked. Rathlin just nodded saying 'yes' in the appropriate places while Angus finished his cocoa. The lad was lost in his own thoughts watching the flames of the fire flicker before his eyes. As soon as it seemed polite to do so Angus and Rathlin sought sanctuary from wedding talk, which was all Miss Puttick seemed good for at present, and retreated to the Turret Room which Rathlin had declared in an aside, as a 'wedding free zone'.

The first thing Angus noticed as they turned to go up the stairs was the sixth Mural that he had never managed to solve.

"I really wish I could have worked that one out and found the dragon," he said pointing to the wall.

"Oh that's Nehebkau, an Egyptian dragon" explained Rathlin.

"Nebecow," attempted Angus unsuccessfully.

"Ne...heb...kau," repeated Rathlin, "It's a tricky one to say... went to Egypt to find him. The clues pointed to him being hidden in one of the Pyramids. Didn't find any trace though and was about to give up when Cyru sensed something. We went outside the pyramid and found this splendid dark green chap. Turns out he had moved on to Dubai to hide in a statue in a fountain... of course he is not the original Nehebkau from Egyptian mythology but he is a descendant."

Angus was open mouthed at the story but even more so as they started up the stairs. Since his last visit new dragon paintings had appeared on the walls leading to the Turret Room. They were much smaller than the original murals that were on the walls of the Great Hall but they served the same purpose. Each canvas pictured a dragon and a clue to its hiding place. If you had no knowledge of the SSDP and looked at these paintings you would think nothing of them other than they were pleasing to the eye, at least as pictures go.

"When did you put these up?" asked Angus.

"Just the other day... Aurora thought it was better to use them... they're portraits of all the newly awakened dragons," explained Rathlin.

"How many have we found so far?" enquired Angus as they continued upstairs.

"Now then," Rathlin paused as if counting in his head, "I think we now have thirty one".

"I can't believe we have found so many dragons," said Angus scanning the paintings, proud of the Society's work.

"Once I'd started to make sense of Finian's notes it was quite easy to find the dragons and awaken them," Rathlin looked at one of the paintings, "Aurora has been a great help with her knowledge and your support has been immense," he finished turning to look at Angus.

Angus thought he recognised some of the dragons he had helped to find. However he spotted some he did not know as they reached the top of the stairs.

"I don't think I know these dragons... who are they?" he asked, throwing an enquiring glance at Rathlin.

"Ah that is Oswin and Leofric... now they were found last month in Norway. They're brothers... found them on a clock tower hiding in two statues near the top," and then laughing, "What a job I had getting them to come down."

"Do they have protectors yet?"

"Oh yes Halla looks out for Leofric and Lars keeps an eye on Oswin... they are siblings as well and like you, very much into dragons... both in their mid-twenties."

"How did you manage to find them... surely the book didn't work in Norway?" continued Angus keen to go there to see the dragon brothers for himself.

"Of course it did... I placed 'Dragonalia' in the main library in Oslo and they picked it up, found the pamphlet just like you." As they began to walk he continued, "It really is a great way of finding new recruits and I am glad you brought my brother's inventive recruitment scheme to my knowledge."

Angus was pleased to hear that and as they walked onto the large landing at the top of the stairs Rathlin read out the strange names and recalled more tales of how they were found. Dragons almost seemed to jump out of their pictures as Rathlin recited names on the way past. As they continued along the draughty corridor Angus heard about Grimbald, Kendrick, Hildred, Swithin, Beorn and Uchtred. He loved the sound of the ancient names and wondered how Rathlin remembered them all. Then he observed one he knew very well indeed. The painting had a plesiosaurus in it, posing near a large loch. Angus knew it was a loch as opposed to a lake because he had been there. It was the hiding place of Nathair the Wyrm and Angus shuddered once again as the memory of the meeting with that unsavoury character came flooding back to him. He realised Rathlin was now a few paces ahead and caught up quickly, still looking at every picture as he went. The pictures had stopped by the time they reached the end of the corridor and at last the step to the southwest turret appeared in front of them.

Entering the Turret Room Angus took a deep breath in anticipation. This was where all things pertaining to the SSDP were kept. For him this was the most exciting room in the castle. He often tried to imagine what it must have been like for Finian foraging all over the world, hungry for knowledge and collecting obscure artefacts about dragons. The first thing he noticed today however, was a new pile of canvases stacked in the corner of the room, ready for hanging on an empty wall.

"So are all these new as well?" asked Angus as he pulled one out from the stack and gestured at a striking drawing.

"Now there's a magnificent beast…black from head to tail and named Felspar," replied Rathlin with admiration. Angus thought he looked very aggressive and moved on to admire a gentler looking one.

"Who's this?"

"Farrell… Found in Ireland and the next one is Gilmor a friend of his hiding close by" explained Rathlin as he started to gather some papers and resume his search for any reference to Barfoot.

Angus continued to leaf through the paintings and found a few others that he had not seen before.

"Do we have protectors for all of these?" he asked.

"Most of them… more and more are coming onboard all the time now".

It still gave Angus a thrill to think that he was involved in this ancient Society, especially one he had actually been partly responsible for its revival.

"Sorry Angus, I have some business to attend to… can you carry on without me for a while? I won't be long," said Rathlin and after a nod from Angus, he left the boy alone in the Turret Room which to Angus was a bit like being unsupervised in Aladdin's cave, with no-one telling you not to rub the lamp! He was particularly interested to see Rathlin's map on the wall showing the locations where the dragons had been found and where the Society had already recruited members worldwide. Each awakening and protector was marked with a coloured pin. As Rathlin had said earlier all the new recruits were found in much the same way as Angus had been, by reading Finian's book 'Dragonalia'. A copy would be placed in a library to be read by enquiring minds and only those truly interested enough in dragons would take the time to find the Pamphlet hidden inside. The Pamphlet invited the discoverer to write to the Headquarters of the SSDP. Rathlin would vet the letters and meet the applicants to decide who was worthy enough to take the oath and thereby be enlisted into the Secret Society of Dragon Protectors. Angus left the busy map and started to roam around the room taking in the piles of documents that they had been sorting through. His eyes fell upon the pile he had been looking through last week when Miss Puttick had surprised him with the news about the wedding. Suddenly he remembered the file he had dropped and placed on top of the filing cabinet for safe-keeping. He walked over and took it down holding it with both hands and at an angle to catch the light. The paper was yellowed with age and had obviously been read many times as it was marked and very dog eared. It was entitled 'Dragon Hierarchy' and he recognised Finian's neat script as he read.

*Nothing much is known about the social order or class of dragons. It is commonly believed that they are loners, shunning all contact from others. This may be a misconception grown from legends that imply that dragons pass much of their time alone in the lair. Contrary to this, evidence suggests that they actually enjoy the company of other dragons and possibly even humans, as long as said guest was not harbouring intentions of stealing or capture. It is entirely plausible that dragons have some sort of assembly, led by an ancient and wise individual whose sole task is to provide the focal point of a civilisation steeped in history and to protect that knowledge, but as yet, this is not proven.'*

The passage went on with a few more interesting details, similar to Finian's thoughts in his book, 'Dragonalia'. However Angus' attention was drawn to the bottom of the document. Written there was one sentence which really stood out. It was scribbled as a note or an afterthought, as if added after the original passages were written. The writing was not as neat or as straight as the rest of the documents script and it was certainly out of context in the passage.

*'Considered their holy grail, 'The Cor Stan' is the real source of a dragon's power and is held in the ancient home of the dragons,' the Birthing Caves.'*

Angus did not understand what he was reading. Just what had he stumbled across? What was the Cor Stan? He had no idea and had never heard of it before. Confused he read on, but there was no more of any further interest. Certainly there was nothing expanding on the meaning of Cor Stan. In fact no mention was made of the Birthing Caves either.

"Have you found Barfoot then?" enquired Miss Puttick from the door.

Angus gave a start, engrossed as he was in the document and its contents.

"Oh Miss P… I never heard you come in," replied Angus slightly flustered. "No I haven't, but I found something else," he answered handing the paper to her. She was silent for a minute while she read Finian's finely written words, slowly raising her eyebrows as she did so. When she finished she looked at Angus with a bemused expression.

"Well it's all very interesting but why has it got you all excited?" she asked.

"Read that bit," he replied pointing to the bottom of the page.

"Oh… so that's it," she said after taking in the note. "Well it is rather strange but so was Finian from what I can tell… It was probably just one of his madcap ideas and based on nothing more than supposition."

"Yeah I guess you're right Miss P... I just thought maybe it was important... It certainly sounded like it was," he conceded dejectedly.

"Well perhaps it is... Let's see if I can translate it..." she replied smiling at the sudden delight in his face. "'Cor' literally means 'heart' and 'Stan' is an Old English word for 'stone'... 'The Heart Stone'," she concluded.

"Heart Stone?" repeated Angus, none the wiser.

"Well never mind I'm sure we will discover what it is once we finish looking through all this," she said casting her hand in the direction of the piles of information still to be sorted.

They were frustrated by their fruitless search for any mention of the name Barfoot and when Rathlin came back to help Miss Puttick resume the heavy task of filing, Angus decided to have a break and go outside to find Pyrra.

After a quick snack in the kitchen he went down to the main cavern where he found his dragon friend conversing with both the oldest resident of Calmor and Cyru, the youngest.

"Hi Cyru... hello Hereward... how are you both?" he enquired politely.

"Oh Angus...found anything on Barfoot then?" asked Cyru enthusiastically.

Angus shook his head gloomily to silently confirm that they had not.

"Well never mind young man I am sure you will find something before my old memory kicks in... blasted hibernation plays havoc with the mind you know," added Hereward sensing the boys dejection and referring to the negative effects the centuries long sleep had on a dragon's memory. Angus remembered how it took Pyrra several weeks to regain her cognitive powers.

He listened as the venerable dragon spoke to the others about his former hiding place. It seemed to be an old country house that had a cast iron gas lamp above the door. He had hidden there for over two hundred years but eventually the ageing house had begun to fall down. When Finian found him the place was all but demolished and if it were not for the former head of the SSDP Hereward would have been crushed by a bulldozer as it cleared the site for a new housing development. Angus' mind began to drift off as the conversation moved on to Pyrra and her description of her hiding place in Piggleston High Street. He was thinking about the written notes he had found upstairs concerning the dragon hierarchy. Angus was intrigued by this Cor Stan, what it was and why had it been noteworthy to Finian?

"Sorry, what did you say Angus?" asked Pyrra bringing Angus back to reality with a jolt.

"Mmmm… what…?" mumbled Angus confused at being asked a question he was not at all ready for.

"Stan… you mumbled something about Stan… Who is that? A new protector?" she asked again with a puzzled look on her face.

"No I didn't, did I?" Pyrra confirmed with a nod that he had and the three dragons were staring at him waiting for his explanation. "It's nothing… Just something I found" he conceded.

"So you did find something then. Well what was it then?" asked Cyru impatiently.

"A reference to something called the Cor Stan," confessed Angus.

"Is that all? Never heard of it," replied Cyru losing interest.

"Miss P translated it for me… she said it means 'Heart Stone'," he went on, looking at Pyrra. "Do you know what that is?"

"Not the Cor Stan but my Mother gave me a 'Heart Stone' when I was younger. It's here," replied Pyrra pointing to the piece of Dragonore glowing on her chest.

"So what... a 'Heart Stone', we all have one," added Cyru.

Smiling at this small discovery Angus turned to look at the blind dragon who appeared to be scratching his chin and was deep in thought.

"What's on your mind Hereward?" enquired Pyrra breaking the old dragon's concentration.

"Eh... Oh nothing... just thought I knew that name Cor Stan... That was all. I was trying to recall the memory but it's gone now," he smiled, "maybe it will come back to me a little later."

"Did you find anything else Angus?" pressed Pyrra who still watched Hereward as if expecting him to do something.

"The note said something else about Birthing Caves... that the Cor Stan was the real source of a dragon's power."

"THAT'S IT!" shouted Hereward so loudly that Cyru jumped up in the air with fright. "The Cor Stan and The Birthing Caves... they are in the same place." The old dragon was more animated and excited than Angus had seen any dragon before. He was positively leaping up and down as he had obviously remembered something very important.

"What Birthing Caves?" asked Pyrra.

"That's where we used to go to nest long before the Great Hibernation… A female would lay and hatch her eggs there, as it was the safest place to be."
He stared into space waiting to hear a reaction.

"So what has this Cor Stan thing got to do with the caves?" asked Cyru.

"When I was hatched, it was there… obviously I found that out afterwards but I remember lots of dragons rearing their young in the caves there. We were free to roam about and that was where we got our 'Heart Stone'." They all stood hypnotised by the milky eyed face of Hereward. "My mother chipped off a fragment of a large glowing stone and taught me how to roll on it to attach it to my soft underside. That stone was the Cor Stan and although all dragons collect precious stones whenever they can, that one was always our first and the most important."

"Wait a minute… Are you saying that this Cor Stan or 'Heart Stone' is the same as Dragonore then?" asked Cyru confused.

"Yes it must be," said Hereward. "All Dragonore comes from the Cor Stan. That is why we wear it. Angus is correct… our power does come from the original Dragonore… the Cor Stan."

"So why didn't we go there?" asked Pyrra, "Cyru and I don't remember it."
Cyru shook his head at Pyrra as if to confirm he did not.

"We just stopped using it after a time… what with humans warring with each other all the time, the expansion of mankind and the ever threatening danger of discovery it became harder to go there… over time I suppose we just forgot about the place as the older dragons died out or started to hibernate," reasoned Hereward sadly.

"So what is this stone? What does it do?" probed Angus excitedly.

"I'm afraid I can't fully remember lad… but it does hold the key to our magical power… without it we would be long dead by now," he said soberly.

"You had better go and explain all this to Rathlin" Pyrra urged Angus, "but we will need to go home soon, so don't be too long".

"Okay I'll see if they've got any further in finding Barfoot," he shouted back over his shoulder just as he started to run off.

"Barfoot was there in the Birthing Caves... I remember him now... he was the Ward... the Guardian of the Cor Stan and the most powerful and respected of all dragons." Angus had stopped dead in his tracks, spun round on his heels and walked back to Pyrra and Cyru. All eyes were on Hereward.

"Are you sure?" Pyrra asked quietly, but she secretly hoped the old boy knew more.
He turned his head in the direction of her voice and seemed to look straight through her.

"Very much so... The cave always had that light blue glow to it. The light came from the Cor Stan... It's him in the dream, I know it!"
Angus was stunned at this news and wondered why the dragons were dreaming about a particular dragon that was probably long dead. Nor could he get the document he had found about the hierarchical structure of dragon society, out of his head. He shook himself from his thoughts and started to run from the cave.

"I have to go and tell Rathlin and Miss P about all this…" he shouted as he sprinted away towards the passageway, "I'll meet you outside Pyrra…" and he was gone, leaving the others looking on, baffled by the stunning revelations.

## Chapter 5

# 'The Lost Mural'

Angus raced up the stairs two at a time to the Turret Room calling Miss Puttick and Rathlin as he ran. He could not wait to tell them of Hereward's recollections. As he headed for the Turret Room Angus was sure he could hear music, he reached the door and without knocking burst into the room.

"Miss P… Rathlin!" he shouted as he did so.
As the door swung inward, Rathlin sat directly in his line of vision but was already rising out of the chair with his hand raised in warning.

"Nooooo…" shouted Rathlin, but the warning was drowned in a cacophony of blaring sixties' music and Angus' shouting. The over-excited lad turned his head to the right just to see the door he had flung wide open crash back on its hinges and into Miss Puttick who stood at the top of a rickety ladder and had been evidently filing the latest batch of sorted documents. It was at that point that everything seemed to lapse into slow motion. The librarian wobbled as the door banged into the ladder. Then she missed her footing on the rung. Flailing and scrabbling for a handhold she tumbled, knocking down books and paperwork as she did so. Angus watched all of this open-mouthed and stunned into immobility as Miss Puttick seemed to hang in the air for a moment. Then things bounced back to normal time as gravity exerted its dominance on the proceedings once more. The librarian made a final lurch for safety, bringing a couple of shelves down with her before finally landing heavily in Rathlin's arms as he leapt headlong in an attempt to break her fall. Volume after volume of dragon notes seemed to rain down on them and the paperwork she had filed flew out of the binders and fluttered down on the betrothed pair like confetti. Angus immediately tried to clear some of the debris to get to Rathlin and Miss Puttick. When he found them they were both crumpled in an ungainly heap on the floor.

"Are you okay Miss P?!" asked a very concerned Angus.

He could see that she had lost her usual composure and was very flustered. Her hair was loosened from its normally tight bun, she had lost one of her sensible shoes and her clothes looked all uncomfortably twisted.

"Ju… Just…" she tried to say whilst trying to sit up.

Angus grabbed her arm and began pulling her upright.

"Arrrghh... watch my hand Angus!" was the muffled shout from beneath the heap of paper and Miss Puttick.

"Sorry Rathlin, I can't see you. Where are you?" shouted Angus.

Both Angus and Miss Puttick began to clear some of the paperwork and found Rathlin's hand, then arm. They followed his limbs until they found his torso and only then did Miss Puttick realise that she was sitting on Rathlin's head!

"Oh I am so sorry Rathlin!" she said as she fretted over him.

"Don't worry about me my dear. Are you okay?" he replied.

From the looks of it neither was seriously hurt and as Miss Puttick fussed about herself, re-arranging her skirt and jacket, Rathlin started laughing.

"And what is so funny? Just look at this wretched mess!" she said as she pointed to the paper-strewn floor. Angus could see she was getting upset and began to say he was sorry but was cut off by Rathlin laughing even louder.

"Now I will have to start all over again! Will you stop laughing!" she said raising her voice in an extremely exasperated manner.

Angus could see she was not really serious as she had half a smile on her face which she struggled to control. Rathlin pretended to compose himself and replied.

"Well it looks like you will have to stay here longer to help me sort it all out, won't you?" he managed before letting another guffaw slip.

"I just might not bother Rathlin Tek... and then where would you be?" she replied trying to sound serious. Just as Rathlin began to believe she was really angry, Miss Puttick snorted then began to snigger. It seemed that she did see the funny side after all as both burst into giggles on the floor, surrounded by bits of paper. They eventually picked themselves up still fussing over each other and laughing at the same time.

"Thank you for breaking my fall with your hard head!" teased Miss Puttick, "You are so gallant," she smiled.

"Why thank you my lady," he replied with a mock bow he could have copied from Argent.

Then they noticed Angus still standing with his mouth open as if about to say something. Only no sound came from his lips. They both looked at him with a little concern.

"Are you okay Angus?" enquired Rathlin with a concerned frown.

"Angus dear... did you get hurt?" asked Miss Puttick when Rathlin's questions went unanswered.

"Uh... oh... I'm fine... sorry, I didn't mean to cause all this mess Miss Puttick. I'll help you file... it ... again..." he replied as he seemed to come back to life for a second before he trailed off again.

All the time he spoke, Angus did not look at the others and instead stood staring at the wall behind the door.

Miss Puttick could see he was mesmerised by something on the wall where the bookshelves had stood. She followed his gaze, as did Rathlin and both of them could now see that he looked at a gap in the bookcase where some of the books used to be. On the wall behind was the merest hint of a faded wall painting.

*Chapter 6*

# *'Krubera'*

Angus stepped slowly forward, cocking his head to one side and squinting at the small part of the wall that was visible. It seemed very familiar to him but he needed to see the whole thing to be sure of what he had already guessed.

"Can you help me uncover this?" he said over his shoulder to Rathlin and Miss Puttick who were suddenly as serious looking as he was. The three Society members started to pull out the remaining volumes from the shelves. The accident and indexing were soon forgotten as they realised what they had chanced upon and were anxious to see more of it. As the books were hastily removed from the shelves the picture on the wall became clearer and clearer. At last the final book was lifted away by Rathlin and he stood back with the others to see what they had found. It was indeed a portrait of a dragon, very similar to the ones in the Great Hall below.

"Any ideas Angus?" asked Rathlin.

Angus knew straight away exactly what and who it was. From what he was told by Hereward it was obvious to him and it also matched his memory of the dream he had as well, a dream that had persisted on returning every night. The mural depicted a stately looking dragon standing majestically in front of a large stone which had a bluish tinge. He had no doubt now and even the passage he had read seemed to make more sense.

"It's Barfoot," he replied at last.

"How can you be so sure?" asked Miss Puttick.

"I'm positive…" he turned to look at her, "I need to explain… after that it will make more sense to you both, but trust me it's him. I know it's him."

A little later they were in the Great Hall, the chaos upstairs and the accident now entirely forgotten. Angus tucked into the flapjacks that had been brought with the tea and he finally got to tell Rathlin and Miss Puttick all that Hereward had revealed. He recalled every word that Hereward had said and then he went on to tell them about the passage of writing.

"Do you see how it all fits together? The dream has been affecting all the dragons and it's Ward Barfoot sending a message about the Cor Stan. He wants to be found. All we need to do now is discover where he is! He is obviously summoning the dragons!" he concluded excitedly.

Miss Puttick and Rathlin exchanged knowing looks.

"Now Angus we don't want you going off on some adventure, and besides you don't know that Barfoot is even alive," replied Rathlin.

"Quite so, it's unlikely that he can be," added Miss Puttick, "and I know what you are like young man."

"How can I? I don't know where the Birthing Caves are anyway!" he said innocently.

"Maybe not now but if you find out you need to let us know before you try to find them," added Rathlin.

"Yes Angus it could be dangerous, and we don't know what that dragon wants," finished Miss Puttick.

"Okay, okay, I get it!" resigned Angus grudgingly. Angus changed the subject back to the mural and who could have put it there. This served to divert the conversation until Pyrra arrived from the cavern below and they finally took their leave of Calmor, settling into the flight home.

Laying in bed that night Angus' mind still reeled, re-running the events of the day. He thought about the mysterious Cor Stan and its Guardian, Ward Barfoot. If it had not been for the accident they would never have discovered the wall painting. No-one knew how it got there or who put it there, but he was sure Finian had known about it and that he was the one who had hidden it. The reason Miss Puttick had started on that bookcase was because it was the only place that had any order. It seemed reasonable to assume that it was Finian who had filed the stuff on those shelves and that meant he knew about the mural. Angus slowly drifted off to sleep and was soon flying above the clouds. This was his favourite dream. He soared downward through the clouds and was suddenly confronted with a mountain range, forcing him to pull up rapidly. His vision seemed to focus on a small cave opening and then his eyesight blurred. He shut his eyes as the blurriness made him nauseous and when he opened them again he now faced Barfoot. The ancient Ward was speaking, only this time Angus could hear him.

"Ge cunnan the answer 'Draca Gast'. Search in the correct place. Nu aweccan Angus!"

Angus sat bolt upright in bed. It was 2 a.m. according to the clock and no way could Angus get back to sleep now. His mouth was dry and he was totally spooked by the dream and its clarity. Barfoot had called his name! Was it really a dream? It had all seemed so real! Angus had not even realised he was out of bed until he put the glass to his lips and tasted the milk. He stood in the kitchen and that was when he saw it, the computer. Why had he not thought of it before? Angus sat down and waited for the computer to whir into life. He logged onto the Internet and found the search engine he wanted. Now where to start? Angus thought about what he knew of Finian's death. He died in a cave-in some three years ago and was in Eastern Europe at the time, but where exactly? He started with 'Finian Tek'. Nothing found! That would have been too easy. He pulled up a map of Eastern Europe and studied it for a while. Maybe something would jog his memory. Okay there was Poland, Hungary, Romania, Bulgaria and the Ukraine. None of them offered inspiration. He studied the screen until his eyes hurt but no memory was jogged by any of the countries there. He moved the mouse pointer to the back button to start another search but just as he did so something on the screen caught his eye. It was the Black Sea. Dermot had once told him that Finian was off exploring in the Black Sea region when he was killed. He went back to the search engine and typed 'Black Sea + Cave-in' then Angus pressed enter. An article from a news website came top of the list and the date was from the time of Finian's disappearance. Angus clicked on the link and the headline leapt off the screen and grabbed his full attention.

# Death of Local Naturalist in Krubera Caves

He quickly scanned the article but there was nothing more it could tell him. For Angus though, this was more than enough. He now had an idea where the Birthing Caves were and he was equally convinced that Finian had been looking for them when he died. In fact Angus had never been surer of anything in his life. He typed in 'Krubera Caves' and found a map and an article about 'the deepest and most inaccessible underground area known to man'... ah but not to dragons, he thought! Angus did not get much more sleep that night, but as dawn approached he finally drifted off with no dragon returning to haunt his dreams.

The next morning he was up showered and downstairs eating breakfast before either of his parents got up. It was Sunday and the only day they did not go driving around delivering Kleanware products. They stayed at home but they would probably stock-take or do some bookkeeping.

"Mum can I use the phone to call one of the boys at school about the homework assignment we have to hand in tomorrow?" he asked after she got up.

"Of course you can dear," she replied, without looking up from the table.

Angus did not want to be overheard so he took the cordless phone outside the front door and dialled the now very familiar number of Calmor. He spoke at length to Rathlin about Krubera and his theory about Finian's mission, convinced that there had to be some link between the caves where Finian died; the originator of the dream, Barfoot and the mysterious Cor Stan.

"Well what do you think?" ended Angus eventually.

"Angus if you don't grow up to be a detective, then I for one will be amazed. How on earth you put all of this together so quickly I will never know!"

Of course Angus had mentioned nothing of Barfoot talking to him in his dream.

"It's all very intriguing that's for sure. I will have to explain this to Aurora and then we will need to plan our next move," continued Rathlin.

"When can we go there?" blurted Angus, instantly regretting it.

"Ah well not until after the wedding. We have to make sure we are organised for such a trip..." then remembering who he was talking to, "Now Angus you must remember

what we spoke about yesterday. Do not go off on your
own!" instructed Rathlin sternly.

Angus made all the right noises without actually promising
not to do anything. He went indoors to replace the handset
and decided he needed to go for a bike ride once he had
done some printing and found his backpack.

Angus arrived at the sweet shop and, after the usual
greeting with cough candy, found Pyrra already at the trees
by the time he had ridden his bike there. He explained what
he had deduced and she listened patiently until he had
finished. He looked at the intuitive dragon who knew at
once, without a single word from Angus, what he was about
to suggest. She smiled, not unkindly, at his attempted
subtlety, as if he was unsure of her reaction and perhaps
fearing she may react similarly to the adults. She also knew
of the dangers but Pyrra was confident they could make
this journey safely and she very much longed to put an end
to the dreams once and for all. She certainly was not going
to wait until after the wedding which was still weeks away
and she correctly guessed Angus was just as keen.

"Well what are we waiting for?" asked Pyrra causing
Angus' face to instantly light up and a smile broader than a
Cheshire cat's spread across it. "I don't suppose you would

have a map and perhaps some information as to our destination in that bag of yours?" she winked.

"Well I did bring some things with me just in case," he grinned whilst searching for the maps he had printed from the Internet.

"I hope you have warm clothes?" she enquired. Angus confirmed this by pulling out some of the stuff he had brought and she nodded in approval.

Pyrra wasted no time in switching to dragon time as they had a long journey ahead of them and several weather fronts to contend with. She rose with ease above the cloud line, stretching her long neck and rhythmically beating her wings. Angus settled into the very long flight. Having read everything he could about the Krubera Caves he realised that the place they were going was actually one of the deepest and most inhospitable cave systems in the world. It had limited access and in some parts it was two miles underground. He had no idea where the caves were exactly or what they were going to do once they got there. Obviously they were limited in what they could achieve. In fact he secretly feared they would find very little or nothing at all, but at least they were doing something and Pyrra needed this distraction. He wondered whether Pyrra had helped herself to any more sheep lately but did not like to ask. He assumed she had eaten something before undertaking such a long journey, especially since she was not getting too much sleep.

It was not long before Angus could make out a great city sprawling below. It was London and as they flew past to the North of it he could not help wondering whether any dragons were hiding there undetected, just waiting for him to find them. Soon they hit the coast and started across the sea to Europe. Angus checked his map, trying to work out the fastest way there. Then he spotted land again and it was obvious that they were passing over the Netherlands. After that it was impossible for him to really make anything out and he got bored with trying. He must have slept, as the next thing he knew was when Pyrra lurched forward and began to descend.

"What's wrong Pyrra?" asked Angus concernedly.

"Nothing... I just thought we could use a break... I know I could," she replied.

"Oh right... eh... of course!" he replied, embarrassed after seeing the desperate look on Pyrra's face. They touched gently down on a hillside near a pine forest and Angus jumped down to stretch his legs. Pyrra walked off to the trees and Angus sorted himself out and put on another jumper under his jacket. He had just eaten some food and now studied his maps when Pyrra came back.

"Would you like a pie or something Pyrra?" he offered.

"No thank you Angus I ate the other day so I will be fine for a while," she replied politely.

"How far have we come?" enquired Angus.

"Well if we are going to Georgia, on the east side of the Black Sea then we are about half way," replied Pyrra looking at the map and pointing to the western-most part of Eastern Europe.

"Wow that far in three hours, you must have been motoring Pyrra!" exclaimed Angus.

"I have not flown much faster, that's for sure. Well, if you're ready?"

They took to the skies once more and Angus settled his head down on Pyrra's back and once again lost himself in his thoughts and dreams.

Some time later he was drawn gently back to consciousness.

"Angus, wake up! I think you will want to see this," called Pyrra over her shoulder.

Opening his eyes sleepily Angus was rewarded with a
wondrous sight. A vast expanse of water stretched out in
front of them, and to either side he could just make out the
land masses although they were partially obscured by the
bad weather they had flown into. It was bitterly cold and
Angus fought to stay warm by clinging to Pyrra as much as
he could. Obviously March was not a time for good weather
in this region. As he studied the water speeding underneath
them he could see some fishing boats jostling with the
stormy sea below. This was a most inhospitable place and
it seemed to get worse as they moved further eastward. A
coastline came into view in front of them. At first it was hazy
and Angus was not sure if it was really there at all. Then it
began to become clearer and a spectacular mountain
range sprang up behind it.

Pyrra began to gradually lose altitude and Angus could
sense that they were getting close to their destination. The
clouds were ominous looking and he was sure that a storm
was about to unleash itself on the mountainside. He did not
think that it would be a pleasant experience at all and
hoped they could find some shelter before it vented its fury.
Pyrra lapsed from dragon time back into normal time and
Angus began to study the mountains as they approached.

"According to the information you gave me Angus it should be around here somewhere, but without a sign pointing it out I doubt we will spot it," said Pyrra, disappointedly.

Angus did not answer as he had been thinking the same thing. He looked up at the clouds again with a real feeling of frustration and then he noticed something strange. Now he knew he was mad! He deliberated for a few moments as to how to approach this and then decided that, with Pyrra, honesty was the best policy.

"Pyrra I think it's over there," he pointed.

"What makes you say that?"

Angus knew that was coming.

"Well it seems to be where that dragon shaped cloud is pointing," he replied, embarrassed as he knew it sounded silly. Pyrra simply looked up, just managing to make out what could be construed to be a dragon fading as the clouds moved across the darkening sky. She turned back to Angus and smiled as she tilted her great wings and bore down on the mountainside near to where the cloud had appeared to indicate. As they did so Angus could see that there was a section just below the snowline that would make a perfect landing site.

The area was a barren place, strewn with rocks and rough grasses. A few bushes were all that could be seen as no trees could possibly grow here. It was the same place he had seen in his dream last night, just before Barfoot spoke to him. The wind howled around the pair as Angus delved into his bag for a chocolate bar and offered Pyrra a 'cough candy' sweet. She did not take it as she was too distracted and very anxious to find and enter the cave. Angus started to search for anything that could be the entrance but apart from the rocks, he could not see any opening. He turned around slowly and scanned the small valley for any possible entrance. He could see some greenery on his left. He started to make his way towards a clump of thorny looking bushes and was about half way there when he spotted a hooded figure. Angus stood rooted to the spot. With no features visible and just a hooded cloak it was impossible to tell what manner of person this was. Pyrra shouted to Angus from the other side of the dip. When he did not answer she came over to see if he was okay.

"What's the matter? Why don't you answer?" she enquired with a note of concern in her creaky voice and watched as he just pointed in the direction of the figure. Pyrra stopped dead in her tracks. Angus could see that her Dragonore glowed and now he felt the warmth on his chest from his own stone hanging around his neck. Despite knowing that this unfamiliar person had Dragonore Angus did not feel any more relaxed about the stranger. Whoever this person was they did not offer a greeting nor make any gesture, they just turned around and walked slowly behind the bushes and out of sight. At first Angus did not move but gathering his courage he skirted around the bushes, keeping at a safe distance. As he did so, the cave entrance appeared before them. He just caught a glimpse of the shrouded figure disappearing into the cave and because of

the ever-growing empathy between boy and dragon,
wordlessly they followed within.

## Chapter 7

# *'Dormant Energy'*

Inside the cave Angus and Pyrra found themselves in total darkness. They tried to focus on seeing whatever might be lurking in the gloomy interior. At first it seemed as black as night and they could not make out anything at all.

"Do you think we can trust this character?" asked Angus.

"I don't know. He would not be the first person to have Dragonore and not be friendly" replied Pyrra in a whisper. They edged cautiously forward and just caught the shape of the shadowy figure walking ahead of them. It was getting too dark now to see anything and Angus fumbled for his torch in the pale and failing light.

"Can you still see?" he asked Pyrra.

"Yes I can... Just! There, up ahead... but he's stopped," she replied quietly.

"How do you know it's a man?" asked Angus as he switched on his torch.

"I don't... I just sense it".

Angus shone the torch around the cave to get a better look at their surroundings. The ceiling of the cave was cracked and craggy as if pieces had fallen away recently, indeed the floor was strewn with boulders and smaller stones. Water had started to run downwards past Angus' feet as the threatening storm announced its intent to thrash the mountainside. This was manifested in the form of a thunderous boom and an instantaneous flash of lightning that lit up the inside just long enough for both dragon and boy to see the cloaked figure standing a little further ahead. Angus moved the beam of light further down the slope towards the waiting figure. The man, if indeed it was a man, was now moving away from them and disappeared around a rock face and out of sight. Pyrra and Angus exchanged glances and started after the hooded figure. When they reached the place where he had been standing they could see that the path suddenly got narrower and steeper. Soon they were descending rapidly and the air was getting even colder than it had been outside. Angus took a deep breath of freezing air, trying to fill his burning lungs with his heart pounding in his chest. He stopped to shine the torch ahead and look for the figure. Again the cloaked person was just on the edge of sight, but way further down inside the cave. Angus was sure that they could not have caught up with him even if they wanted to. Pyrra pointed her nose to the left.

"Watch your step Angus," she said.

Angus swung the torch round and instead of a rock wall the light went into yawning blackness. They were on the edge of an open crevasse which disappeared down into the impenetrable darkness beneath. To Angus it looked like an endless abyss and indeed that was not far from the truth. It took him a few seconds to get over his fear and slowly he began to move very carefully down the slope to the last place where the figure had stood. When they got there the cave was a dead end and nothing could be seen of the hooded figure. Angus flicked the torch around, shining the light in every direction but nothing was visible except for damp rock and stone. After a while, Pyrra tapped her fore claw on Angus' shoulder.

"Look at this wall," she said.

"What about it?" he asked, but then he realised that it shimmered.

"Do you see it?" asked Pyrra.

"Yes," replied Angus as he stretched out his hand to the wall.

As he did so the wall shimmered more, as if Angus' hand was a stone falling into a pool of water and causing ripples to race outwards from the point of impact. Angus felt nothing peculiar as he continued to push through the wall. He had shut his eyes just before his head passed the point the wall appeared to occupy and after taking one step he quickly opened them again. The seemingly fearless lad was dumbstruck at what he had just experienced, Pyrra stepped through to join him and she too stood in awe of the sight that met them.

Angus switched off his torch as it suddenly occurred to him that he no longer had need of it. Both adventurers looked down the long cave in front of them. The shrouded figure was nowhere to be seen but it was obvious that he could only have gone in one direction. Angus' eyes adjusted to the strange new light inside the cave. It slowly dawned on him that there was light in the cave, although he noted that it was not daylight and it had a strange bluish radiance. It was the same pale light he had seen in his dreams and it gave the rocky interior an eerie hue. He wanted to tell Pyrra about it, but since he had not told her about his experience with Barfoot's message he decided to keep it to himself for now. The long cave stretched like a tunnel in front of them. It was almost level, although here and there it undulated slightly. As far as Angus could see the sides were rough rock, as was the ceiling, but the floor seemed to have been cleared with most of the bigger rocks pushed to the side. He noticed that the centre of the tunnel floor was worn smooth as if well-used. He strained his eyes as far as he could see and it looked as if the tunnel bent round to the right some way up ahead. He could only guess that it plunged deeper into the heart of the mountain. Angus then followed Pyrra's gaze as she scanned what was now a solid rock wall behind them.

"Come on Angus. There is only one thing for it, we must keep going forward," said Pyrra jolting Angus from his contemplation.

He nodded and stayed close to Pyrra, gaining courage from her size and weight. Empowered by each other's presence the pair edged their way forward and with every step Angus felt himself become, not only stronger, but somehow more energised. He looked at Pyrra and the Dragonore on her chest seemed to be glowing more fiercely than he had ever seen it before, even in the presence of many dragons. In fact his own was now very hot but not burning his skin. Angus reached to his neck and pulled the strap that held the pouch he kept his Dragonore in. He held it up and he could see the stone glowing through the small bag.

"Do you feel anything Pyrra?" he asked nodding to the Dragonore on her chest.

"Yes I do. I feel fantastic actually. Stronger than I have for a long time," she replied fervently. "Do you feel it as well?"

Angus nodded his affirmation to her question, leaving her looking thoughtful and after stuffing the pouch safely back under his t-shirt they set off along the tunnel once more.

They followed the passage for what seemed like ages

until at last they could see an opening with a larger cavern behind. They both paused for a second or two and Angus noticed that the intensity of the Dragonore was now very strong indeed, leaving him feeling almost euphoric. They edged forward to the end of the tunnel and peered into the most magical place that Angus had ever seen. The floor sloped downwards from right to left. The cavern was not very high, certainly not as high as the sanctuary back at Calmor. The right side of the cavern had a smoothed but uneven floor interspersed with pillars of rock that had formed from dripping stalactites into large stalagmites. On the left more stalactites of various sizes became increasingly numerous until they looked like a field of barley hanging upside down. They pointed into a pool of glassy water that seemed to reflect the whole cavern like an enormous enchanted mirror. The entire scene was bathed in the pale bluish hue and gave the impression that they were looking at some enchanting grotto from a fairy tale. Both of them were so taken by the beautiful sight before them that they had unwittingly stepped forward a few paces without realising it. Shaking himself from his reverie to focus once again on the task at hand, Angus quickly scanned around the cavern for any sign of the shadowy figure. He could see nothing but then he noticed that the cavern had many tunnels and niches further on. It seemed to Angus that the entire place was a labyrinth and that they would surely get lost if they went further within.

"Do you notice it is not cold anymore Angus?" asked Pyrra.

Angus had been too awestruck to notice the temperature but now that she had mentioned it, he was warmer and started to take off his backpack and jacket.

"Do you think these are the Birthing Caves?" he said looking at Pyrra to confirm what he believed to be true.

"I have no doubt you have brought us to the right place, but apart from this stranger we have followed I can see no other sign of life," she replied, "However my 'Heart Stone' tells me that something else is nearby and I must find out what," she finished.

Angus and Pyrra made their way cautiously through the pillars and past the mirror pool to the far end of the cavern. They did so they could see that the place was enormous as it opened up into many other passages and caverns that had been previously hidden from sight. They stood in the middle and glanced from opening to opening, trying to work out which way to go. Angus pointed to one that seemed to glow slightly brighter than the others.

"I think we should try that one first," he said to Pyrra. Pyrra already knew that Angus was a very extraordinary boy but sometimes she thought there was even more to him than was plainly apparent. She shook the thoughts from her head and moved towards the entrance he had chosen.

As they reached the mouth of what was yet another cavern, but much smaller and plainer than the one they were leaving, they were at first blinded by a light that seemed to intensify just as they reached the opening. They stood for a while shielding their eyes from the glare whilst they tried to recognise some sort of detail within the interior. The brightness gradually subsided and from the growing shadows they began to make out the shape of the object projecting the light. A large stone, about the size of a dragon's body and perhaps half its height, dominated the cave room. The rock was obviously the source of the penetrating light and seemed to pulsate as they edged towards it. As Angus approached he

could see that it was very rough and uneven and that small shards were lying on the floor below its resting place. The pieces on the floor were glowing as well, and when he looked at Pyrra, her 'Heart Stone' or her Dragonore, glowed in the same fashion. Angus was speechless; this surely was the Cor Stan and he could not believe they had found it! The Dragonore around his neck felt warm against his skin and when he looked up at Pyrra her eyes were glassy with tears. To the dragon it must have felt like coming home. They seemed to stand for ages gazing in wonder at the stone, but it was probably only a few moments. Dragon and boy were completely mesmerised by the blue light which was a force of supreme energy emanating from deep underground. Suddenly a voice broke through their reverie, and both Angus and Pyrra spun round.

"Welcome my freonds to the Birthing Caves ac the ham of the Cor Stan. My name is Ward Barfoot."

*Chapter 8*

# '*Failing Light*'

The voice had come from the doorway of the chamber
which was now filled with the imposing figure of Barfoot.
Angus instantly recognised the dragon from his dreams and
he was truly puzzled by the fact that he, Angus, had not
only shared in the dreams that the dragons had been
having but that he had also received what seemed to be a
personal message in his sleep. Although obviously very
old, the dragon standing in front of them neither sounded
nor looked as ancient as poor Hereward. In fact Barfoot
had a sort of radiant aura about him, making him look
positively regal. Centuries of hibernation had not aged him
as much as it should have and Angus wondered how much
of a part the stone had played in keeping him in such good
health. Barfoot was only slightly bigger than Pyrra and at
first Angus thought he was the same colour as the Cor
Stan. He was in fact white, and once Angus realised this he
could only marvel at the unusual albino like appearance of
the dragon. Apart from his jade green eyes he was almost
translucent with no other markings.

No reply was forthcoming from the two amazed visitors but, despite this, Barfoot stood quite still surveying them with his mesmerising eyes, patiently waiting for them to recover their composure. Pyrra was the first to regain her wits and speak.

"Halettan Barfoot, I am Pyrra and very happy to have found you," she replied politely, "I trust the dreams will now stop, as we have answered your summons?"

"I was na lost Pyrra... It is eall other dragons that were lost," replied Barfoot sagely.

Pyrra stood looking confused at this statement giving Barfoot the opportunity to further expand.

"The gameatan... my apologies I have not... mastered the modern Englisc completely yet... The dream was designed to aweccen the dragons... We have slept for too lange, and the time has cuman for our cynn... kind... to start libban... living again," he explained in his strange mixture of Old and Modern English.

As Barfoot completed this explanation his eyes fell on Angus and, feeling obliged to say something, Angus introduced himself.

"Hi, my name is Angus... Will the dream stop now?"

"Yes I ceased sending the dream last night once I knew you were on the way 'Draca Gast' and furthermore I am pleased that you were the one to find me Angus," replied Barfoot as if speaking to an old friend.

"But we have never met… have we?" replied a very confused Angus who struggled with some of the words being spoken by Barfoot, especially things like 'Draca Gast', whatever that was supposed to mean.

"All will be revealed through time Angus… for now let us just say that I cunnan… know… you and the honour is all mine," replied Barfoot bowing slightly to the stunned lad. Pyrra looked on, confused by what she had just witnessed and made a mental note to speak to Angus about whatever he had been hiding from her, as she was obviously missing something here. She quickly put the thought to the back of her mind as she caught sight of the hooded figure behind Barfoot. Barfoot noticed her distraction and glanced back at the entrance to the cavern. He offered an explanation of this new presence.

"That is 'The Watcher'. He came to the caves some years ago and awoke me from my Hibernation," said Barfoot gesturing towards the hooded man.

"But who is he?" asked Angus, keen for a proper introduction.

"Let us just say that for his own very god... good reasons he does not want to be sceawian... looked upon... ac I must biddan you both to respect The Watchers wishes to remain anonymous ac to ignore his presence... he will hearm... harm no-one ac is a peaceful man," replied Barfoot with enough firmness to suggest that there was no option.

"Of course we will... but can't you tell us anything about him?" Angus implored.

"He has been my gefera... companion... for some time ac has been a mæst eðnis... great comfort... to me... When he first arrived there was a large rock fall ac he was badly hurt. I was alerted to him ac brengan... brought him here." Barfoot glanced in the direction of The Watcher and motioned to him to come forward before continuing. "He has gained mægen ac miht... strength ac power... from the stone ac remained patiently nearby helping me with my English ac informing me of the way the world now is" finished Barfoot as The Watcher blended once more into the shadows of the cave interior. "It was shortly after that

time that I was aware of other awakenings befeallan…
happening".

"How could you have known about that?" enquired
Pyrra forgetting The Watcher at once.

"Through the Stan…" answered Barfoot pointing to it, "It
has a mæst miht … greater power than you can
asmeagan… imagine… as you will now forstandan…
understand." He walked towards the Stone and continued
with his story. "I have been guarding the Cor Stan for four
thousand years ac it is indeed the efne ac bysen… only…
source of Dragonore…" Barfoot stopped at the foot of the
Cor Stan and turned back to his captivated audience. "I
cannot tell you where the stone originally came from but
what I do cannan is that it is thought to have fallen from the
rodor… sky… during a meteor shower some five hundred
thousand years ago… The stone itself gives us our special
powers ac… and radiated a formerly intense, but now
fading blue light." Barfoot paused for a second as if
recalling a certain sadness that troubled him. "You see the
Stone also draws its own strength from the proximity of
dragons as well as giving out powers to dragons close by…
It's a sort of symbiotic relationship between two natural
forces."

"Whoa awesome!" was all Angus could think to say. Pyrra stayed silent waiting for Barfoot to continue.

"Since before the Great Hibernation there were no dragons returning to the Stone ac it went out of memory and hige... thought... its own powers began to fade ac that was part of the problem..."

"Hereward told us that dragons stopped coming here to nest because of the difficulty of the journey and then the Great Hibernation started... the dragons went off to hide until the world became a better place to live in," interjected Angus.

"That's correct Angus ac during the Hibernation they had no need to return to the Birthing Caves... I myself was the last of the Wards guarding the Cor Stan. After I was alerted to the aweccans... awakenings I sent out the message to all dragons via the dream to tell them to 'return' but I did not count on them having problems understanding what I said or remembering where the Birthing Caves were."

"How old are you Ward Barfoot?" enquired Angus using his full title.

"I have greatly benefited down the centuries from my close proximity to the Cor Stan, which had enabled me to live for over six ac a half thousand years".

"Indeed I am honoured to be in the presence of such an elder," said Pyrra very reverently and bowed her head to Barfoot.

Angus could only guess that it was the dragon's way and stood quietly by.

"Thank you Pyrra. You show the proper respect ac your mother Ailith taught you well."

"You remember my mother?" replied Pyrra incredulously.

"Yes and I gemunan… remember Hereward as well, in fact I remember all the dragons that were born here ac when I die that ongytenes… knowledge… will be passed onto the next Ward. It is part of the power the Stone instils to the Ward." Barfoot once again looked saddened and added, "But now my light is failing ac I will in fact forðferan… die soon."

"No, we've only just found you! You can't die now! Surely we are here to save you!" blurted out Angus.

"I am sorry Angus but it will happen soon ac I must prepare for it… that is why I brought you here ac it will be my last task as Ward to choose a new Guardian to take my place, as sentinel of the Cor Stan."

Pyrra and Angus were again open-mouthed in their speechlessness. A silence enveloped the cave and none of the trio spoke for what seemed like ages.

"How do you go about choosing?" asked Angus, his thirst for knowledge at last getting the better of him.

"Well that has been dictated in ages past by Trials ac it is over four thousand years since the last."

Barfoot lay down beside them and bade them to sit on the stone floor. Angus picked up a shard of Dragonore and toyed with the glowing rock whilst Ward Barfoot went on to explain more about the Trials.

"You see, several dragons will be picked from the willing participants ac they will then take part in Trials that will test their skills in many ways… It is only the truly worthy that will win through to the end ac take the place of Ward. Once that is done I will be able to pass on the mantle to another ac die in peace," finished Barfoot.

"So that is why you sent the message to us all… you knew that you were soon to die!" Pyrra spoke in a reverent whisper.

Angus thought it was unlike her to be overawed by something and guessed that to a dragon this must have been a bit like meeting royalty.

"Exactly so," affirmed Ward Barfoot.

Pyrra looked absolutely heart-broken by the news and could not hide her disappointment.

"Do not be disheartened Pyrra," said Barfoot in response to seeing her sadness, "You will come to see that this is but a niwe anginn... new beginning for us all... Your journey has yet to fully onginnan... begin, ac both of you are very important... Remember that" he said wisely.

Ward Barfoot studied Pyrra, smiling at her and when she looked at him she began to smile back.

"That is much better... now I expect you are wondering why I brought you here... I have an important task for you both."

He had their full attention now.

"I gather the SSDP is back in business and working well?" They both nodded. "Good! Now you must take all that I have told you back to the SSDP ac explain what has to be done. The dragons must be brought together so that it can be decided who will take part in the Trials. It would be best if the leader can come here to see me as I can then explain everything properly… Will that be possible?"

"Rathlin wouldn't miss this for anything..." replied Angus eagerly. Then as an afterthought he added, "cept maybe his wedding," he added sheepishly.

"Please tell him ac bring him here as soon as you can… I do not have much time left and the Trials must take place in a few months."

Ward Barfoot stood up and wished them a safe and swift journey home. They took their leave of him and retraced their steps. They followed the mysterious Watcher back through the tunnels guiding them silently to the shimmering cave entrance to the surface. They stood blinking in the sunshine, relieved the storm had passed. Worthy of his name they felt The Watcher's unseen eyes boring into them as they departed from the basin on their long flight back home. He watched until they were no more than specks in the sky before then turning and disappearing back into the bowels of one of the deepest caves known to man, and dragon.

*Chapter 9*

# 'Countdown Started'

The flight home was uneventful. It was obvious to Angus that Pyrra was thinking about Barfoot and everything he had said. He could understand her distress, having just discovered the venerable dragon only to find out he would soon be gone forever. Pyrra seemed to be flying faster than before as she sped time up for herself, allowing the world around them to apparently slow down as if to a standstill. She must have felt some benefit from being so close to the Cor Stan.

"How does Barfoot know you Angus?" asked Pyrra completely out of the blue and pulling Angus from his own thoughts.

"He doesn't… at least I have never met him in person," replied Angus hoping that she would believe that much, as it was sort of the truth and he really did not want to tell anyone about the dreams just yet.

"Never mind… it just seemed that he knew you… perhaps he does because of the Cor Stan… who knows what powers that has given him?"

'Enough to send me a personal dream', thought Angus to himself.

"We will pick up your bike and head straight to your house as it's getting very late and I don't want you to get into any trouble."

"Thanks…," was all Angus could meekly reply.

It was not until they stopped off at Angus' home that he realised that Pyrra must have flown extremely fast as it had taken them nearly six hours to get there and only four and a half to get back. When Angus entered the house his parents were watching TV in the living room.

"That you dear?" shouted his Mum from the couch.

"Yeah Mum. Sorry I'm late. Got a puncture on the way back but managed to get it fixed," he replied, hoping that they would not ask too much more.

"I was just starting to worry about you…" she went on with his Dad shaking his head exasperatingly, behind her back.

"Sorry," conceded Angus whilst trying to conceal a smile at his Dad's antics.

"Not to worry dear, your dinner is in the microwave… Just heat it up when you're ready," she finished with a smile before turning back to the show they were watching. Now that she mentioned food Angus realised he was famished and throwing off his jacket he proceeded to gulp down his dinner as fast as he could.

Later Angus lay on his bed and looked at the ceiling. He was thinking deeply about what to do next. Should he call Rathlin, risk his wrath and try to explain to him on the phone? Or should he just wait until next weekend and go with Pyrra to Calmor? All he knew was that he was desperate to tell them the news, but at the same time he knew that both Miss Puttick and Rathlin would be most upset with him. After a few minutes more debating with himself, he decided to call them tomorrow night and get it over and done with. Surely they could not be too mad, especially once they realised he had found the Cor Stan, Ward Barfoot, put a stop to the dreams and got back in one piece. Not bad for a day's work! By the time he seen them next Saturday, they would be calmer. It was too late to call now and anyway he had school in the morning. OH NO! He had forgotten about school. He dived off the bed and started hunting for his Geography homework which had to be handed in tomorrow. All thoughts of the impending grief he would receive from Calmor went out of his mind as he began to read the neglected assignment.

**Name three countries that were formally part of the USSR and write a short essay about their geographical location, area, population and any other relevant criteria that will help build a picture of that country.**

Angus started to laugh and set off to check the Internet history on the computer for his Krubera search last night.

The Monday night phone call to Calmor was just as he imagined it to be, and as soon as he had explained everything to Rathlin the anticipated response arrived with a vengeance.

"ANGUS HOW YOU COULD GO OFF ON SUCH A DANGEROUS ADVENTURE ALONE I WILL NEVER KNOW!" ranted Rathlin down the phone.

"I know but Pyrra really wanted to go and we were never in any danger, honest!" pleaded Angus.

Rathlin despite his angry concern was secretly impressed with the boy's fearlessness and a little bit jealous that he had found Barfoot. He managed to convince Aurora, who had been bending his ear during the entire conversation that, no harm had come to the intrepid lad.

"Okay so you say this Barfoot wants me to go and visit him to discuss these… Trials?" confirmed Rathlin once

Aurora had ceased her tirade concerning the boy's foolishness and thoughtlessness.

"Yeah that's right... he wants to go over how dragons will be chosen and to discuss when and where it will all take place."

"Okay. You will have to be my guide, so Cyru and I will meet you and Pyrra at Long Reach next weekend. We can set off from there. Say around eight in the morning?"

"Yeah I'll be there," he replied.

Angus could not believe he had got off so lightly, but now he had another problem, he would have to come up with a very good reason for leaving home so early.

It was nearing the end of March and with the wedding now only a couple of weeks away, Miss Puttick had her mind on things other than dragons. Rathlin eagerly seized the diversion given to him by Angus, considering himself out of his depth when it came to wedding plans and come Saturday morning he was already waiting for Angus and Pyrra when they landed in the garden at Long Reach House.

"Ah splendid! You're on time... all we need now is Cyru and we can be off... Now where has he got to?" finished Rathlin testily.

"When did you arrive?" enquired Pyrra.

"CYRU..." bellowed Rathlin at the house, "Oh last night..." he replied hurriedly whilst keeping an eye out for Cyru. "I wanted to break up the flight a little and all Cyru has done this last week is sleep... CYRU HURRY UP!" he yelled again, causing Pyrra to wince.

It was just as the increasingly irate Rathlin had started to stride toward the house that a rather grumpy Cyru strolled from round the side.

"Okay keep your ponytail on! Can't a dragon get freshened up in his own time in the morning?" said Cyru with his cheekiest smile.

Angus smirked at Cyru's jest about Rathlin's striking hair style. He had long white hair pulled into a ponytail. Without further ado, they mounted and set off into the morning sky with Pyrra leading the way and Cyru struggling to keep up. In fact so much so, they had to stop twice on the way to allow Cyru a breather and it was seven hours later when they came tired, but thankful, to a halt in the hollow that seemed to be gouged into the side of the mountain. They made their way down through the initial caves and when they came to the shimmering wall and walked through, Rathlin was beside himself with excitement, much as

Angus had been. All the way along the tunnel he spoke about how ingenious the disguised entrance was and theorised about how it worked. This monologue continued relentlessly until they reached the large cavern with the mirror pool and from then on the wide-eyed, open-mouthed Rathlin said nothing until they reached the cave containing the Cor Stan.

"Stone the crows!" was Rathlin's exclamation at the sight before him. The Cor Stan stood in the middle of the cave with Ward Barfoot slightly in front of it and to one side stood The Watcher.

After making introductions Angus and Pyrra took their leave to explore the caves by themselves and left Rathlin with the venerable guardian Barfoot. The Ward instinctively trusted Rathlin as a man who had dragons' interests at heart and both of them appeared to get on well with each other. The Watcher stood to one side of the room but did not leave as he had done previously. Instead he stood and, true to his name, he quietly kept his eyes on the visitor. If the head of the SSDP had been aware of this scrutiny he certainly did not show it as he, like Angus had been before him, was in awe of Barfoot and the impressive Cor Stan. Pyrra and Angus meanwhile discovered that the cave system was extremely large and only managed to view a handful of the chambers. It seemed a shame to Angus that they were all empty and when he commented on this to Pyrra she simply said,

"One day they will be full again."

Angus did not doubt her foresight for one minute and he sincerely hoped that he would be privileged enough to see it happen.

As they arrived back at the Cor Stan, Ward Barfoot was just giving Rathlin a large chunk of the powerful stone to take back to Calmor.

"This will help you with the selection process at The Behealdan… Gathering… All you need do is place it in the centre of the cavern you described to me and it will ceosan… choose… the participants once they are assembled," explained Barfoot.

Angus noticed that Barfoot's Modern English had improved and that he was not confusing as many words as he spoke.

"The day before the wedding is the perfect time to have The Gathering as everybody will be there," suggested Rathlin. "That's only two weeks so the message will have to be passed on very quickly… I trust I can rely on you two to help with that?" he said looking round at Cyru and Pyrra.

Both dragons nodded their heads to confirm that they would.

"After the contestants have been chosen they will need time to prepare themselves before taking part in any of the Trials," explained Barfoot.

"What sort of training will they need Barfoot?" asked Rathlin. "I will have to pass on this information to allow both dragon and protector to train properly."

"Protector?" exclaimed Angus, barely able to hide his delight.

"Yes Angus. Rathlin felt that the hleo... protector... should be included in the Trials as well... It will make the test harder and a truer reflection of the dragon's skills" explained Barfoot.

Angus could not hide his glee and as he looked at Pyrra he hoped with all his heart that she would want to take part and indeed, be chosen to compete.

"Cyru will be looking to participate with Rathlin, so I will not reveal the tasks to you now... That would not be fair... But speed, stamina, strength and agility will be essential. Above all, the future Ward will have to have full control of their mægen... powers, allowing them to be one with themselves, their protector and the environment around them," declared Barfoot.

"So the Trials will take place in July… this will allow everyone concerned three months to get into shape," added Rathlin.

"Yes and then we will see something that has not happened for four thousand years… The Trials of the Cor Stan!" announced Barfoot solemnly.

## Chapter 10

# 'The Gathering'

With the meeting between the two concluded Rathlin was satisfied he had everything he needed to proceed to the next stage and took his leave with the others. They all returned to the surface, talking excitedly about what the possible Trials would be, and hardly noticed that The Watcher had followed them all the way. As he made his way back to Calmor, Rathlin was filled with an overwhelming sense of well-being and calm, despite his forthcoming wedding. It was as if he had drawn strength and peace from the stone itself. Indeed both Pyrra and Cyru flew in tandem, as they had taken to the air with apparently renewed vigour and strength. Again they made it back home in what seemed like record time and they were both eager to spread the news amongst the other dragons, allowing The Gathering to commence!

Rathlin was anxious to be out of Miss Puttick's way during the run-up to their wedding, so using the Trials as an excuse, he sometimes travelled with Cyru to visit dragons and pass on the news of the impending Gathering. He was not always able to get away and as the Groom he had to spend a fair amount of his time helping Aurora with the preparations. Rathlin did not really mind this as long as she managed to keep her temper. Things like 'the caterer on the mainland not giving her what she wanted for the dinner menu' did not help one bit. In reality it was left up to Cyru and Pyrra to traverse the world informing all the awakened dragons of the discovery of Barfoot and passing on wedding invitations to their respective protectors. The fortnight leading up to the day of The Gathering was extremely dull and boring for Angus. He had to spend most of his time either studying for school tests he would sit after the holidays or running around delivering leaflets and cleaning product orders for his parents. The highlights of the two weeks were when he managed to travel with Pyrra to deliver invitations or when he was able to hitch a lift with her to Calmor. Even then everybody was too busy to speak to him for long and he felt in the way.

Eventually the day arrived when Angus had to pack his bag for the wedding and his Mum fussed around him making sure he had everything he needed, such as clean shirts and socks. Miss Puttick had spoken with her the week before and told her that Angus was to go to her house and that she would travel to Calmor with him. She never said what mode of transport they would take! While Angus found the last few things he needed to finish packing, his Mum went downstairs to find out what his Dad was doing. Angus grabbed his backpack and the holdall his Mum had given to him and followed her downstairs. As he reached the bottom of the stairs he could hear his Mum and Dad talking animatedly in the garage. Evidently a drama was unfolding and Angus was not too sure he wanted to find out what it was all about. Dropping his bags at the front door he walked through to the garage. The garage door was open and a large white van pulled away from the driveway having just delivered a mountain of packing boxes of various sizes. His parents obviously had a problem with what was, by the noises his Dad was making, a large quantity of late orders delivered all at once. Angus' parents were panicking as they were not only behind with their scheduled tasks but they now had to sort all of this lot before they could deliver them.

"There is nothing else for it dear, he will just have to stay and help…" he heard his Dad say.

"But Donald you said it was okay and he is so looking forward to it. You can't do this to him!" she pleaded.

"Do what?" asked Angus. His parents spun around to face him so quickly, that they startled him and caused him to almost fall into some of the many boxes that filled the garage, and most of the driveway.

"Angus, your Father has some bad news dear!" and she waltzed out of the garage very upset, after giving her husband one last angry glare.

Angus looked from his Dad to his Mum and then back to his Dad.

"Well son… It's like this… We need your help with unpacking all this stuff". He swung his arms in the direction of the boxes. "Sorry but it looks like you won't be going away after all…" and again as if it made it better, "Sorry about that… it can't be helped".

Angus let the words sink in, at first not registering what his Dad had just said. His Dad must have thought that his silence was some sort of stubborn show of will.

"Now come on son… It's not that bad… It's only a silly wedding," he cajoled, trying to get Angus on his side.

"IT'S NOT A SILLY WEDDING AND I HAVE TO GO!" shouted Angus as his temper exploded at his Dad's insensitive statement.

"Now don't you take that tone with me young man, we run a family business here and you will just have to jolly well get on with it… Now start with those over there and I will get your Mum to call Miss Puttick to let her know." Angus glowered at his Dad all the way out of the garage and then kicked one of the boxes. Why could they not have normal jobs like other parents? Of all the children at his school, he was the only one who had to put up with this kind of hassle. Deliver this, collect that, sort this, he hated it, and now he could not even get away to warn Pyrra…

"PYRRA!" he shouted involuntarily as he realised that she would be waiting for him at Miss Puttick's cottage. The story about meeting Miss P at her house before travelling to Calmor was not strictly true. He was actually meeting Pyrra there and, once he had called his Mum, they would both fly to Calmor. Miss Puttick was already at Calmor organising the wedding and now he had no way of getting to Pyrra to tell her what had happened! Angus stood and kicked one of the boxes and resigned himself to the task by roughly throwing the boxes from outside into the garage.

One hour later, an invisible Pyrra strutted up and down outside Miss Puttick's cottage. She was getting increasingly worried and the ringing noise from the house was not helping either. Although dragons do not wear watches they can tell the time very well from the position of the sun and the stars and she knew Angus would not let her down if he had a choice. Eventually, anxiety got the better of her and she set off to fly the short distance from Miss Puttick's to Angus' house. 'It's not like him to be late', she thought as she landed gently in the driveway. Pyrra was just about to look into the upstairs windows when her attention was drawn to the garage. A box suddenly appeared, spinning through the air and hit her on the tail. She stood stunned for a second at this strange occurrence and then bent over to read the label on the box. As she did so, another one hit her on the back of the head. Pyrra peered under the garage door, rubbing the back of her head, and could hear someone slamming around, kicking boxes and muttering to themselves. Just as she about to call out another box appeared from within and smacked her right on the snout!

"Ouch!" she cried, as the corner had jabbed right into the bone.

"Pyrra, is that you?" asked Angus from behind a large stack of boxes.

"Yes it is!" said the dragon, still rubbing her head and now her nose.

When Angus materialised from behind the boxes he was met with the face of a cross-eyed dragon, twitching her nose to see if it was okay. Of course Angus started to laugh very loudly indeed and this did not amuse Pyrra one bit.

"Come on… why are you hanging about here? We have to go!" the dragon snorted.

As usual she was invisible and inaudible to humans who did not have Dragonore. However Angus' vociferous laughter had caught the attention of his Mum and she approached the garage. What she saw made her stop dead in her tracks. Her son apparently talked to himself whilst he loudly banged boxes. In fact, he not only muttered to himself, but was having a full scale conversation with… well, with nothing. At least nothing but the garage door, which was open and the only thing in the direction he kept looking in.

"Look it's no good…..they won't let me go until I finish sorting this lot and this will take forever to do!" he said to the garage door.

"Well I'll help you then" replied Pyrra sticking her head and front claws through the opening of the garage and emptying the contents of a box on the floor.

"No...stop...you have no idea what you're doing," shouted Angus at the door.
His Mum could see Kleanware products and packages throw themselves from their boxes onto the garage floor while Angus flapped around shouting at the door and trying to put them back in again.

"Stop!" Angus shouted, "You're being more of a hindrance than a help and now I've got to put this lot away!" he growled unhappily.

"Well, we have to think of something... Miss Puttick will be so disappointed if you don't show up and if we don't go soon I'm going to miss The Gathering, which I really do want to attend!" Angus' Mum did not hear this exchange, only her son apparently arguing with himself.

"I'm sorry... I just can't do it... My Dad won't let me and now I feel I'm letting everybody down." He finished by sitting on a box with his head in his hands, no longer scowling but looking thoroughly dejected.
Angus' Mum had seen enough and thought perhaps they'd been a bit harsh on the lad. If Donald would just stop

whatever he was doing and help her in the garage, perhaps between the two of them they could make up the orders and do the deliveries by themselves.

"I just can't get away… you'd better just go yourself… don't worry about me," he said, again to the garage door.

"Angus love, are you feeling OK? Does Miss Puttick's wedding mean so much to you dear?"
Angus jumped up and looked at Pyrra then to his Mum again. He hoped that Pyrra was invisible and that he would not have to explain why a large green dragon stood half inside their garage emptying boxes all over the place. Angus could only nod such was his fear that, any minute, his Mum was going to run screaming into the house.

"If it's not too late I guess you can go after all… I will sort your father out... and I couldn't get Miss Puttick to answer the phone anyway, so she might still be waiting for you" she said smiling fondly at him.

"Thanks Mum…" shouted Angus leaping to his feet and giving her a rough hug and then he turned to the door again, "I'll meet you at Miss P's house!"

"Is… the door going with you love?" asked his completely bewildered Mother.

"Of course not Mum... doors can't fly" he replied forgetting himself as he ran into the house to grab his bags, leaving his confused and deeply concerned Mum scratching her head and wondering about her son's state of mind. Angus rode off on his bike and promised to call from Miss Puttick's cottage once he got there. He did this shortly before he locked the front door using the keys Miss Puttick had given him and then walking around to the back of the cottage he found Pyrra admiring the flowers in her garden.

"Finally!" she exclaimed, "I hope we can still make it on time."

Three hours later Angus and Pyrra touched down inside the main cavern of the re-opened sanctuary for dragons and stood in wonderment at the sight that met them. There were dragons of all shapes, sizes and colours. In fact the place was so busy that for the first time ever Pyrra had to wait before flying through the hidden entrance because another dragon was flying out. This was going to be an interesting day! Angus passed amongst what seemed like a myriad of beings in the abnormally crowded cavern, soaking up the atmosphere of strange voices and a whole range of colour. There was a general buzz of excitement in the cave as potential entrants and protectors conversed with each other, all trying to second guess what would happen today and what tasks the Trials would involve. Angus was amused by some of the suggestions as they seemed very far fetched, especially the two young men he overheard as he passed them.

"My guess is that we'll need to do some sort of obstacle course with swinging ropes and bags that will knock you off your dragon... you know just like that Gladiator thing on the television!" said the tall brown-haired man.

"I'm telling you they will have us flying to the moon to collect some Dragonore... apparently that's where it comes from!" stated the short curly-haired man with a funny little moustache. Angus had to suppress his laughter and move on very quickly. Old Hereward lay in a dark corner and enjoyed the highly charged atmosphere, but felt his age somewhat as his fragility made him feel a bit out of things. He was all but ignored by the younger dragons and Angus watched Pyrra making her way over to speak with him. Then Angus spotted Georgina as she talked to Godroi and Argent. He was just admiring her brooch when she looked up and their eyes met, forcing him to look away quickly. Angus did not dare to look again for some time, such was his embarrassment at being caught gazing at her. After a

few minutes he felt a little braver and risked another glance. She was now deep in animated conversation with an older boy who was with a spikey black dragon, which Angus guessed to be Felspar. Whilst the two were chatting Angus managed to watch this interaction without seemingly looking, but his attention was increasingly drawn to the black dragon Felspar who strutted around full of self-importance and sizing up the competition. Angus had an inexplicable uneasy feeling about him but brushed it aside as Georgina caught his eye again and drew the tall lad's attention in his direction. Her companion was as tall as Angus' Dad with long straight dark hair worn in a lank grungy style. He had a pale complexion and was dressed in black denims, with a baggy, dark grey t-shirt emblazoned with 'Marillion' the name of some rock band. Georgina, with a wry smile, called Angus over.

"Angus, this is Fergus. He didn't believe me when I said it was you!" she smiled knowingly.

Angus looked up at the face of the tall lad standing before him and tentatively shook the hand offered to him.

"Hey Angus, how's it going?" said Fergus warmly.

"Okay... What about you?" replied Angus, unaccustomed to the twinges of jealousy he felt.

"I've heard all the stories about you but I thought you would be... well sorry... but a bit older and a little taller maybe!" continued Fergus still smiling and seemingly standing a little straighter, as if to emphasise his height.

"Eh... well I'm normal height I guess," replied Angus weakly.

"It's amazing that you were able to do the stuff you did... surely it's not all really true?" persisted Fergus.

"Depends what you've heard," replied Angus guardedly. He noticed that Fergus kept glancing at Georgina as if waiting for her to applaud but she was not smiling and did not seem to be as taken with Fergus as he had first feared.

"Yes it is true... Angus didn't tell the stories. They came from Rathlin!" replied Pyrra from behind Angus, "and I was there!"

"Oh... okay... well Felspar and I have been practising a lot lately so I will look forward to beating you in the Trials, if you get picked," retorted Fergus and with a confident wink to Georgina he sauntered off in the direction of the black dragon, Felspar.

"Who was that…rragh?" asked Pyrra watching him with a look of distaste on her face.

"A what?" replied Angus questioning the strange growling noise that he had come to recognise as the dragons' own language.

"Oh nothing… it is not a very nice word to call someone but it fits him well," she answered angrily, "I saw you talking to him after I had been speaking to Felspar and let's just say they are two peas in a pod!"

"I'm sorry Angus… He seemed quite nice at first and when he asked about you I thought it was just to say hi," said Georgina apologetically.

Angus had felt a bit discouraged by the meeting but as Georgina had spoken to him she touched his arm and an electric shock ran through him. Just as Angus started to feel a bit better, Georgina's father Hugh called her over to where he, Godroi, Argent and Rhys were all standing and rather reluctantly she left Angus with Pyrra.

Angus composed himself, glanced around and noticed a few dragons he did not know. Some of them he could guess from the paintings that Rathlin had shown to him.

Certainly Felspar's image was unmistakeable. With over thirty hibernating dragons now found and awakened, Angus scanned the room for others he could recognise. As he did so, he spotted a dark green dragon that really stood out. Not only was it slightly different from the rest in terms of appearance, but the boy standing beside it was dressed in Middle Eastern clothing. Angus realised that this must be Nehebkau and his protector from Dubai, if he recalled Rathlin's story correctly. Angus decided to try and introduce himself to the boy as he looked a bit lost.

"Hi I'm Angus, pleased to meet you" he said, offering his hand to be shaken in what he hoped was a friendlier manner than his last conversation.

"Assalam'alaikoom, I am very pleased to meet you Angus, my name is Kadin," replied the boy who looked very exotic in his long white robe and a white cloth draped over his head held in place with a black rope. Angus suddenly felt rather shabby next to Kadin who was positively immaculate in radiant white.

"This is Pyrra and I take it you are Nehebkau?" Angus continued with the introductions, "I have heard all about you from Rathlin."

"Indeed… and we you" replied Nehebkau bowing his head slightly.

"I don't mean to be rude, but why are you are slightly different from the other dragons?" asked Angus sheepishly.

"Ah, that is because I am an Asian dragon… in fact, the last Asian dragon to be found… I am afraid all of the rest have now left this world."

"I am sorry to hear that," replied Pyrra. "Was there not an ancient tale of how they went in search of another universe that they could be safe in?"

"Yes there was, but I'm afraid that it was nothing more than a myth. I have searched far and wide but found nothing to suggest that any are still in this world or any other for that matter," answered Nehebkau sadly.

Angus was intrigued by this new information and wondered if it was possible for the dragons to do this but he was distracted by Kadin who was going on to explain how Rathlin had met Nehebkau and then recruited him.

Just as Kadin finished his story, Rathlin called for their attention. He stood in the middle of the chamber turning to everyone and patiently waiting for silence to prevail over the first assembly of the SSDP for more than three hundred years.

"Ladies and Gentlemen, welcome to Calmor..." he looked around smiling broadly at the many faces now focused on him and waiting to hear his every word, "Firstly I would like to say that never have I been prouder to see so many magnificent creatures in the one place... and that the dragons are quite splendid as well..." Everyone laughed but Hugh Penfold simply doubled up and applauded so loudly that everyone began looking in his direction, embarrassing Georgina immensely and forcing her to elbow him in his side.

"Be quiet Daddy!" Angus heard her shush through her forced grin.

"Now to the business at hand..." continued Rathlin trying to drown out the guffawing Vicar, "As you all know I have been to see the venerable Ward Barfoot in Georgia. He was the focus of great distress recently whilst he haunted your dreams giving all of you many sleepless nights."

"I would say!" cried a few of the dragons.

"However, thanks to the relentless enthusiasm and bravery of one person, Barfoot's whereabouts were discovered and the mystery surrounding the message was solved... that person was none other than Angus Munro!"

Angus did not expect this at all and as he scanned the beaming faces in the circle they had made around Rathlin, he could see that everyone clapped and cheered him. He did not know whether to laugh or cry, such was his embarrassment! He smiled weakly at the faces around him and could see that neither Fergus nor Felspar were clapping nor cheering but simply scowling in his direction. Then he spotted Georgina smiling at him and his face went even redder than before, if that was at all possible. After a few more agonising seconds studying his feet; something he seemed to be doing a lot of these days; the noise subsided and Rathlin started talking again, allowing Angus to look up at last.

"And now to the matter of the Trials" he continued speaking in a confident manner; a man at ease amongst friends. "As many of you already know the Trials themselves will not take place until the month of July, giving all candidates three months to hone their skills…"

"What skills do we need to hone exactly?" asked Felspar, in what sounded to Angus like a very bored and low growl.

"Well unfortunately I don't exactly know, but all I can tell you is what Ward Barfoot told me…" Rathlin paused as if trying to remember the exact words and then as if reciting from memory, "You will need speed, stamina, strength and agility. You will need to have full control of your powers…"

"Is that all?" interrupted Felspar mockingly.

"Ah no… you will also need to show that you are one with yourself, your protector and the environment around you," completed Rathlin, taking pleasure in wiping the smug look off Felspar's face and causing ripples of conversation around the cavern.

"C'mon Rathlin surely you have more than that?" shouted Argent above the increasing din, "You're holding out on us!"

The Vicar shushed him noisily and this seemed to quieten everyone else at the same time as the focus reverted back to Rathlin.

"I have no more to tell you!" said Rathlin firmly, causing more outbursts of 'that doesn't help' and 'I bet he knows it all'. "I know nothing more that the rest of you as Cyru and I are hoping to compete as well. So it's no good questioning me further as Barfoot told me only what I have made known to you today. I can assure you that all will be revealed twelve weeks from now."

"Where?" shouted out the short curly haired man.

"That will be disclosed the day before the start of the Trials, as I wish to protect the whereabouts of the Cor Stan until the last minute."

"But we are dragons… we have a right to know," snarled a fiery red beast from the opposite side of the circle to Angus. As he watched the beast growl menacingly at Rathlin it occurred to him as he glanced back at Felspar, that just like humans not all dragons were good.

"I realise that this might not be to everyone's liking but these are my instructions," bellowed Rathlin, now looking impatient and pressured. "For now, let us commence with the selection process."

## Chapter 11

# 'The Choosing'

Murmurs of agreement rippled around the cavern and the odd 'hear, hear' or cheer rang out.

"I discussed with Barfoot what is to happen and how the choosing ceremony will be done. To complete the task he has given me this!" and with a swift movement, similar to that of a stage magician, he removed the black silken sheet that covered the large rock Barfoot had given to Rathlin. An original piece of the Cor Stan! Silence descended on assembled members of the SSDP and their charges. All eyes were firmly fixed on the largest piece of Dragonore most of them had ever seen. Angus glanced over at Georgina and her eyes glittered brightly, wide-open in wonder. Even Fergus and Felspar were mesmerised by the glare that replaced the lights of the cavern as the stone gave off its eerie blue light that to caressed everything in the cave.

"I now call upon Hereward to announce the manner of the choosing as decreed by Ward Barfoot," pronounced Rathlin's voice breaking the spell. Hereward, as the oldest and most revered dragon at The Gathering, was invited to stand beside the large fragment of Dragonore. He slowly dragged himself with much effort into the middle of the cavern, foregoing his usual dark corner and solemnly placed his claw upon the incandescent stone. At first Angus could not make much out but then he began to hear the low growl Hereward made. It was largely unintelligible to the human audience as the old dragon intoned in the ancient dragon language, but Angus was surprised to find he could grasp the odd word. The stone began to glow fiercely and soon Angus struggled to look at it. Whatever Hereward was doing it was somehow connecting with the Cor Stan. Or at least the chunk of it they had before them. Angus felt the heat from his own Dragonore hung around his neck and he could see that all of the dragon's chests were gleaming brightly where their 'Heart Stones' were placed.

"Can all of the protectors step back and allow the dragons to step forward?" said Rathlin quietly, as if not wanting to disturb Hereward, who now had his eyes closed but still chanted with serious concentration. The dragons did as they were bid, each focusing on the glowing rock, which seemed to draw their gaze as it increased in intensity. Angus watched from just behind Pyrra and he could see all the other dragons he knew so well. Godroi and Argent were just off to the right, side by side as usual. Cyru was not far from them standing next to Rhys, she looked unhappy and Angus remembered that she did not want to enter the contest despite the persuasive pleading of both Cyru and Argent. Between the two pairings stood what looked like the siblings, Oswin and Leofric. Both of them were very much alike and Angus would not have known who was who, had it not been for the protectors standing behind them. Next to Angus stood his newly-made friend Kadin, with the Asian dragon Nehebkau. Felspar was at the far side of Cyru and his blackness was menacingly enhanced in the pale blue light of the stone. Farrell and Gilmor stood on the left of Pyrra and although Angus could not remember all the names he did recognise Hildred, Swithin, Kendrick and Beorn. After that came Macklin, the angry looking fiery red dragon, with the American boy Chad. Angus had never met them but Rathlin had spoken about them. One or two others he did not know, flanked Macklin, and on the opposite side he could make out Grimbald and Uchtred. When all dragons were in position, Rathlin walked to Hereward and touched him on the arm. This must have been a signal because as soon as this happened Hereward began to chant even louder and the sounds seemed to change. At first nothing seemed to be happening except for the hairs standing on the back of Angus' neck. The stone was no brighter than before but no-one dared to move for what seemed like minutes but was in reality only a few seconds. Suddenly a beam of light burst from the stone moving erratically left and right, it was just like a search light Angus had seen in a movie about a wartime prison escape. The light continued to flash around randomly for a few seconds until Angus realised that it had fixed itself on Gilmor's Dragonore. That beam stayed in place as the original beam continued to circle unpredictably, fixing another beam on Cyru and attaching itself to his 'Heart Stone'. Two more fixed themselves on Leofric and another whose name Angus had forgotten. The beams continued to fix themselves onto the chests of Nehebkau and Godroi. Angus wondered just how long it would continue when he realised that Pyrra had a beam on her 'Heart Stone'. Inwardly he leapt with excitement at the thought of what he could look forward to, but then he noticed that Felspar and the red dragon both had one as well and this took the edge off his joy. It was then he realised that Hereward's chanting had stopped and even though the stone's light was slightly diminished, the beams

still held in place, like lasers. Rathlin took notes as he
scanned the circle of dragons.

"Can I ask the dragons that are not chosen to please
step back?" he said as he continued to write.

As the unsuccessful dragons stepped back beside their
protectors, Angus could not help but notice the contrast in
Rhys. She was positively ecstatic about missing out, which
was the opposite of poor Argent, who looked crest-fallen
and absolutely miserable. Of the thirty or so dragons now
under the protection of the SSDP only ten were left held in
place by the beams of light connecting them to the stone.
Rathlin looked round the chosen dragons and checked his
list. It was obvious that he himself was happy as he raised
his hand to calm the chatter from the others and once the
noise died he began to speak.

"The stone has decided who will compete," he smiled
happily, "The contestants will be Oswin and Leofric…
congratulations both of you… Macklin…" the American boy
with the enraged looking red dragon whooped and jumped
around, "Nehebkau… Farrel… Gilmor… excellent!" he
applauded, encouraging everyone else to do the same,
"Godroi… Pyrra…" Angus applauded with his hands above
his head and shouted 'Yeah' as Rathlin continued,

"Felspar… AND last but not least CYRU!" cried Rathlin as he shouted the last name; obviously delighted himself that Cyru was chosen and therefore allowing him to compete as well. The cheering and applauding grew louder and louder. As this happened Hereward, who had still been chanting away quietly, stopped. The beams of light suddenly disappeared and Angus observed that this released the dragons from the stone. Pyrra turned to him and he could see that she was overjoyed at being picked. The cheering began to quieten down, although Angus' attention was again drawn to the red dragon Macklin when both he and the boy with him taunted Cyru, saying they were going to wipe the floor with him. Protectors and dragons alike praised the lucky ones and everyone began talking at once breaking into noisy groups, offering congratulations and commiserations.

Angus moved off with the others as they filtered out from the cave, the chosen contenders busily discussing their theories on what the tasks may involve. Amid the general hustle and bustle Hereward moved further into the sanctuary of his dark corner, he had had enough excitement for one day. He listened to the sound of the others leaving and began to retreat back into his cave at the very end of the cavern. The light from the stone had been hurting his poor eyes, the required chanting had exhausted him and he felt some peace and quiet, and a good sleep, were just what he needed to restore himself. Feeling his way, more from memory than anything else, he settled down into the most comfortable corner he could find and closed his eyes. His thoughts were drifting off to times of old and the memories of colour he once had before losing his sight and it was during this that he realised something was wrong. Everyone had left the cavern but he felt his Dragonore glowing, which could only mean that there was still a dragon or a protector left in the cave. He opened his eyes again and was about to shout out, however something was not quite right and his dragon instinct told him to lie low. He strained his ears listening with all his might to gain some knowledge of what was going on. His breathing was shallow and almost non-existent in his effort to become completely silent. Still nothing came to him and from what dim shadows of light his eyes did allow him to see, there seemed to be no-one nearby. Just as he begun to think he had imagined the presence, he heard voices… a human one first… scared and timid.

"But what if we get caught… found out?"

"WE WON'T… Didn't you look at them?" sneered a dragon voice, "Not one of them is a match for me… I am the natural choice as leader. I am smarter and stronger and I will make sure of winning… even if it means killing one of them…"

"No you can't!"

"BE QUIET… I need that stone… and I will have it, and all the power that comes with it… I will be the greatest and most powerful dragon, forcing the others to my will…" Hereward shifted his weight and bumped a loose rock causing it to clunk off another one. "What was that?" growled the angry-sounding dragon voice.

Silence blanketed the dark cave and Hereward dared not breathe, such was the effort he made to be still. Then Hereward heard the voice again. Only this time it was full of malice and bad intent, such as he had not heard in thousands of years.

"Someone is here… leave now… I will deal with this!"

## Chapter 12

# *'Ash & Stones'*

The ceiling above Angus was whitewashed and framed with Celtic carved oak beams, stained dark over the many hundreds of years they had been set as the backbone of the castle. Of course he did not know this and as Angus was still half asleep, it took him a few moments to remember where he was. The events of the night before started to seep back into his mind, as slowly he regained his wits and shook the sleep from his body. After The Gathering everybody buzzed with strategies and theories on what they obviously knew nothing about. The group Angus was with talked into the small hours of the morning about Barfoot, the Cor Stan and how it all came about. He was happy just to listen to his dragon friends as they discussed what preparations they would have to make for training and was pleased that, as Godroi was there, he had a chance to spend some time with Georgina.

As the night wore on, the groups dwindled away as most of the protectors and dragons flew home together. Only a few were staying for the wedding the next day and Angus noticed that Fergus stayed until late with Felspar at his side, speaking with various other clusters of humans and dragons. He was glad that they had not sought him out for conversation nor would they be at the wedding either. There was something about Fergus that Angus just did not like, possibly it was the way he showed off for Georgina, and as for Felspar the black dragon, he was just arrogant and rude. That last thought of Felspar jolted Angus completely from his sleepy stupor and with a rush of sudden energy he threw back the covers and leapt out of bed.

It was a glorious April day at Calmor, freshened by a sharp shower and the spring sun that was now warming the day. Rathlin had awakened early and he breathed in the delicious scent of the cleansing rain, mingled with the island's own peculiar smell of aniseed. Somewhere in the back of his mind Rathlin recalled a quote from Chaucer. He wondered why he had suddenly remembered it, especially since it was from his schooldays. Must be the poetic mood he was in, after all it was his wedding day!

"Whan that Aprill with his shoures soote, the droghte of March hath perced to the roote..." Rathlin recited aloud to himself in the mirror.

He could not quite remember the rest and gave up after taxing his memory for a few seconds more. After one last lung-full of the tremendous heady mixture of scent that crept in through his open window, Rathlin reverted to the task of getting ready for the biggest day of his life. He whistled as he dressed and ran his eye over the wedding preparations already faultlessly arranged by Miss Puttick into a list for him.

As the morning wore on guests and dragons busied themselves by helping to prepare the food and the Great Hall for the ceremony. Angus arrived on the scene feeling rather full, having just come via the Kitchen where he 'quality tested' a few items which would be served later to the wedding guests. He watched as Georgina fussed around her father who was clumsily assembling a makeshift pew at the far end of the hall near the great doors. Miss Puttick was nowhere to be seen as she had hidden herself in one of the other turret rooms like some fairytale princess. She was very particular that Rathlin did not see her before the service began. Rathlin himself was having trouble with his tie and at the same time trying to organise the dragons into the spaces dictated by Miss Puttick's instructions. A few of the other protectors were running around moving tables and chairs and generally getting in each others way. It was after some time that Angus realised Georgina was standing next to him, also surveying the madness from this vantage point.

"Are you busy?" she asked smiling cheekily.

"Yeah… I mean… No!" stammered Angus, "Sorry, not really I was just…"

"Yes I know… Miss Puttick is not going to be too pleased when she sees this mess," she cut in, finishing Angus' attempted assessment of the proceedings.
He stood tongue-tied and embarrassed by his inability to speak.

"Can you come and help me with something? You would really be doing me a favour," asked Georgina.
This was more like it. 'Action… I'm comfortable with action' thought Angus. He nodded his willingness to help and soon found himself laying tables, carrying in plates and bringing in the wedding cake, which he was relieved to place finally on the table after dodging several dragons' tails. Things were starting to take shape now and as it was nearly midday, it was soon time for the wedding to start.

"Angus can you make sure everyone is ready and can you please ask Pyrra to organise the other dragons?" pleaded a harassed Rathlin.

Angus noticed that Georgina had disappeared as he asked people to stand in two flanks on either side of the Great Hall. Pyrra and Cyru manoeuvred the other dragons into position behind the protectors. Everyone was finally in place and Rathlin stood fidgeting nervously beside the beaming Hugh Penfold. Angus quickly surveyed the congregation again, looking for Georgina. He spotted her at the bottom of the stairs and when she noticed him, he was rewarded with a warm smile which made him blush. She waved to her Dad the Vicar and after a nod from him she ran back upstairs. Angus satisfied himself that everyone was where they should be before taking his place at the front. He looked over his shoulder anxiously checking to see if Georgina had returned when suddenly she was beside him and gave him a friendly poke in the ribs from his blind side which caused him to jump.

"Sorry I didn't mean to scare you," she giggled.

"No… you don't scare me… didn't scare me," he stammered in reply.

She gave her father another wave and he motioned to Dermot who in turn placed the blowpipe of his Uilleann pipes into his mouth and began to puff into the bag. Angus thought his face looked rather funny as it was puce from the effort of blowing so much and his cheeks were all bloated like a puffer fish. At first it did not seem like Dermot could play and the bagpipes wailed and screeched loudly causing some of the dragons to shift uneasily. Then the notes began to flow together and suddenly Angus could hear a recognisable tune. Dermot played, standing proudly in his kilt, which was made of a pale earthy green plaid, and wearing a tweed jacket. The tune was called 'Rab's Wedding' and it slowly caressed the assembled wedding guests. Angus thought it was very apt for the setting. He realised that everyone was looking back and he could see Miss Puttick coming slowly down the stairs and into the hall. Angus was stunned as she was dressed in a long plain ivory silk gown and looked almost ethereal. Her hair, normally screwed up in a bun, flowed freely around her shoulders and there was a circlet of Blue Dragon Fire in her hair. Angus had never seen her look more radiant and it was a far cry from her usual librarian attire. She walked… no, she floated slowly to the entranced Rathlin, down between the two rows of dragons as they sniffed, appreciating her aniseed circlet. Angus could not help but think the dragons looked like an honour guard, the largest he had ever seen. She smiled secretly as she passed him and joined the waiting Rathlin in front of the Reverend Hugh Penfold. Angus could not concentrate on the exchange of vows, which he found boring as it held no interest for him at all. Or the hymn singing, as all he was really conscious of was his burning cheeks at the close proximity of Georgina. Pyrra meanwhile loved it, a great social occasion and another chance to catch up with her friends. Angus could not help thinking, that if there were a hat-maker for dragons, Pyrra would surely have gone for the biggest and most outrageous! Everything about the ceremony went off very well; Hugh Penfold made a great and jolly speech about...well Angus had no idea. He was not concentrating on anything except trying not to look at Georgina who stood far too close to him for comfort.

After the service, the Vicar came to reclaim his daughter and Georgina gave Angus a quick peck on the cheek before disappearing into the throng. He did not know what to do after that and just stood there trying to figure out if the embarrassment was too painful to bear or whether he was in fact deliriously happy. The trance was only broken by Argent, as he bumped into Angus whilst he showed off to Pyrra and Rhys. Everyone enjoyed themselves tremendously, dragons and protectors alike. The cake was cut; the bouquet tossed and caught by Rhys. The speeches and toasts were brought to a close and Angus began to feel a little more relaxed in Georgina's company. Cyru was trying to show one of the other dragons how to play football with a stolen table cloth that he had rolled up and tied into a make-shift ball. Angus laughed as the blue dragon tried to kick it and only succeeded in getting it stuck between his claws.

"It's a pity Hereward can't see the fun!" he chuckled to Georgina.

"Oh yeah..." she replied and looking around the room she continued, "where is he, I haven't seen him all day?"

"Come to think of it, neither have I..." pondered Angus, "Maybe we should ask Cyru if he's sick or something." It did not take them long to find out that Cyru had not seen him either. In fact after asking around it became quite clear that no-one had seen Hereward since the end of The Gathering. He and Georgina decided they would go and look for him and although Angus fervently hoped the old dragon had not come to any harm, he had a nagging feeling that something was wrong. He was distracted from these thoughts when he realised that he would be alone with Georgina for the first time. They made their way down into the deepest part of Calmor, the nesting cavern, where they had held The Gathering the day before and talked about the wedding and the SSDP. Angus knew that bright light hurt the blind old dragon's eyes and so he expected to find him in one of the caves or niches at the far end of the cave system. Walking across the cavern floor to the other side Angus could not see any sign of Hereward and he led Georgina over to the cave where he had first met the old dragon. The inside was pitch black and they progressed into the darkness, Georgina took his hand as they stumbled over the uneven floor. Instinctively he steadied her and he felt her hand squeeze his.

"Why would he come down here?" asked Georgina unnerved by the silent darkness, "It's creepy."

"He likes it… his eyes hurt with the light," replied Angus feeling more confident by the minute.

Suddenly they heard a faint and low groan coming from the very end of the cave passage. Angus could not exactly pinpoint where it originated but it seemed to be coming from deeper inside the cave. It was far too dark to go any further without aid.

"That's him… but he doesn't sound too good… We need a light… Let's go back and get some torches," said Angus leading her back.

A few minutes later they were back using the torches to scan the interior of the cave for any sign of Hereward. At first Angus could hear nothing and he called out a few times but to no avail. He was about to give up when he heard the groan again. It was fainter than before but it was enough to point him in the right direction. Angus moved slowly in the direction where he thought the sound came from and nearly stepped into a steep and narrow chasm that suddenly opened up beneath him. Angus shone the torch into the gloom below and could just make out the crumpled grey shape of something wedged into the gap, some twenty feet below.

"Hereward is that you?" shouted Angus into the black void.

At first he heard nothing and was about to move on when he heard another groan. He shone the beam back to the indistinct shape below and was rewarded as Hereward managed to lift his head slightly.

"Down here Georgina... we've found him!" shouted Angus.

The old dragon moaned again just as Georgina arrived at his side.

"Quick, we need help... Go and get Pyrra and tell Rathlin what's going on... and tell him to bring some rope."

It seemed like an eternity before the others arrived and when they finally did Pyrra tried to communicate with the old dragon. She listened carefully to the low growls and translated that he thought he had broken his wing and maybe some other bones. He then went quiet and they assumed that he had passed out. They were worried about getting him out now, as he would not be able to help them in his weakened state and it was very narrow gap indeed.

"I think our best hope is to fashion a large sling with rope," explained Rathlin, "then we have to try and secure poor Hereward in it."

"How will we be getting to him then? That's a very narrow gap sir... too small for the likes of us..." said Dermot dejectedly.

"I'LL DO IT!" shouted Angus without hesitation.

"Are you sure Angus?" asked Rathlin seriously, "I don't know how deep it is and it will be very dangerous."

"I know… but he needs help now and we can't wait…" Angus glanced down at the inert shape of Hereward, "Let me do it… please!"

Having volunteered to be lowered down into the chasm to try to secure the trapped dragon, Angus was made ready for the descent. Being smaller and more agile than the any of the others he was perfect for the job. Rathlin urgently tied knots in a strong piece of rope, forming a double loop. He showed Angus how to pull the loose end once he had fastened it around Hereward's body. Rathlin gave Angus the sling which he looped over his shoulder. Soon he was being lowered inch by inch down the rock face by Rathlin who had tied another rope round his own waist and groaned as he took the boy's weight. Angus called out when he reached Hereward, but could barely find any foothold and it was obvious that the chasm still went down for some metres. The injured dragon seemed to fill the hole and Angus swayed just above him.

Somehow Angus, all the while dangling in the chasm, managed to loop the rope cradle around the stricken body of Hereward. It took him several minutes and he slipped more than once giving not only himself but Rathlin a fright, but eventually he pulled the loops tight and managed to use his jacket to protect the damaged wing.

"OK, he's secure!" called Angus up to the others.

"Stand by Angus, we will pull you up first," replied Rathlin. "Pyrra, Cyru can you take up the strain on Hereward?" called Rathlin to the other dragons. Rathlin, with renewed strength, managed to extract Angus from the dark hole, while Pyrra shouted support to Angus. When they were ready, the dragons at the top braced themselves, and on Rathlin's command, they very gently began to pull Hereward to the surface. At first he would not budge but with Rathlin calling instructions to Hereward, who seemed barely awake, and telling the others when to pull, they soon had him free. They laid the broken dragon carefully on the floor of the cave. His watery eyes fluttered as the old dragon drifted in and out of consciousness. They stood around looking at each other, not really knowing what to do next when Hereward opened his eyes wide and growled so quietly that Angus could barely hear him. Pyrra moved nearer to hear what he was trying to say. He muttered something with urgency and great effort, obviously in a lot of pain. Goodness knows how long he had lain there. The Dragonore on his chest started to flicker and lose its luminosity. Pyrra, in her wisdom, knew what was happening and she told everyone to stand back. The Dragonore flickered intermittently for a few seconds and then went out just as his weak eyes closed for the last time.

Angus knew the old dragon had passed away and he felt a lump in his throat. What he had not bargained for was what occurred next. The lifeless shape that was Hereward began to smoulder as smoke began to rise from the body. At first Angus thought he was seeing things, but small cracks of blue light began to show up in his scaly hide. As the seconds went by they became brighter and more numerous, until it seemed that his entire body was lit from the inside, by a bright blue light. Angus could see that his mouth had begun to glow outwards and then the dragon's body burst into small blue flames. Hereward combusted in front of them and the bright flames grew in intensity until Angus had to shield his eyes, as did the others. When he turned to look again the last of Hereward fizzled for a moment and fell into a mixture of ash and precious stones on the floor. Angus retrieved his jacket from where it lay smouldering and shook it a couple of times. He was stunned by what he had just witnessed. He heard a faint sobbing next to him, and turning, he instinctively put his arm around Georgina who was crying.

"So that's why no-one has ever found any dragon bones!" he whispered in awe, then added; "Pyrra, what was he trying to say?"

She sniffed hard next to Cyru, both of them staring at the place where the old dragon had been only a few seconds before.

"Don't trust him," was her barely audible reply.

*Chapter 13*

# 'The Hazards of Dragon Flight'

A few weeks into their training, Angus watched Pyrra going through her paces as she practised her flying skills at the other Tek estate, Long Reach. When he had looked for somewhere Pyrra could train, he remembered the avenue of poplar trees behind the house. They had once gone to look for Cyru there and Angus thought it would be the perfect place to perform some of the more tricky flight manoeuvres. It had taken Pyrra a while to come to terms with the death of Hereward and she now appeared to have put the sad episode behind her. With the Trials to look forward to, Angus was pleased to see she was much more like her old self.

The two friends enjoyed being in each others company and really looked forward to the long, but much needed, exercise session ahead. In spite of the serious nature of their visit to the old Tek house, Angus could do nothing to curb Pyrra's sense of mischief that morning and she instigated a prank at the local shopkeeper's expense, just as she had on a previous visit. The old man unloaded fresh bread from the delivery van and the feisty dragon, taking advantage of her invisibility, could not help homing in on his peaked cap and knocked it off in a daring swoop that exposed the poor man's bald head. There was not a breath of wind in the air and the grocer could not understand what had knocked it off, as he bent down to retrieve it for the third time. The unseen duo were doubled up with laughter.

Eventually, Angus asked Pyrra to set him down by the chestnut tree on the Tek estate, to formulate a training schedule for the day. He undid his backpack to look for a notebook and pencil, but as he rummaged in its depths he found a chocolate bar instead and eagerly bit into it. Pyrra seemed more fired up than usual and did not want to rest just yet.

"I'm going to do some more laps," she shouted as she sprang athletically from the ground.

"What's got into you?" shouted Angus after her, but she was already flapping her great wings so hard that he doubted she could hear him.

Pyrra launched into the air, to gain height by flying vertically and then, like an old spitfire fighter plane from the Second World War, she dipped her head, shaped her body like a dart behind her out-stretched neck and dived headlong towards the ground. Like a rocket she plunged earthward and just as Angus thought she might have left it too late, she flicked her wings and flattened out, ready to fly through the trees at a greater speed than she had ever tried before.

The feisty green dragon carried on practising faster and faster. She almost clipped her wings as she swerved in and out of the tree line whilst the boy watched, fascinated, from the shade of the solitary chestnut. He marvelled as Pyrra swooped and soared through the closely planted trees, she became as streamlined as she could and increased her speed with every circuit. He clicked the button on his watch. That was another second off the time.

"Excellent Pyrra... keep it up!" he shouted at her as she swept past for yet another lap.

He was proud of her progress and could not wait for the Trials to begin. Angus sensed his Dragonore glowing and he looked around to see Rathlin walk towards him carrying a strange leather contraption.

"Ah Angus, I thought I might find you here," he said proffering the gift.

"What is it?" enquired Angus perplexed.

"Would you believe it's a dragon saddle? I found a couple of them in a trunk in the attic and presume by the shape and size of them that they were actually used by my ancestors for riding dragons," Rathlin explained, whilst he tried to hold up the saddle, as if the effort would help Angus recognise it for what it was.

"Are you sure it's safe?" asked Angus sceptically, "It looks a bit ancient if you ask me!"

"Rubbish!" replied Rathlin indignantly, "with a few modifications and a bit of spit and polish, I think this could be just the job!"

Angus was still dubious about the saddle and seeing this Rathlin offered more assurance.

"It could be what we need to harness some of that dragon speed, and more to the point, to make sure we don't fall off in mid-manoeuvre," he laughed.

"Well... I guess you could be right," conceded Angus.

"Anyway, there are two of them, so if you want to try one, it's yours. I'm off to find Cyru to test mine and if they work, I think we might make some for the others!" called Rathlin, as he strode to the front of the house.

Angus was left pondering the ancient leatherwork as he held it up and tried to figure out precisely which way it would sit on Pyrra's back. He was not even sure that she would be happy enough to wear it. After all as she often reminded him, she was not a horse. Pyrra must have spotted the contraption and already hovered over him with her wings spread out wide on either side of her body. She allowed her body to effortlessly float down to the ground next to him.

"Great landing Pyrra... what do you make of this?" he asked as he showed her the strange object.

"An old saddle by the looks of it... I haven't seen one of those in centuries... where did you get it?" she enquired.

"Rathlin found it in the attic and thought maybe we could use it... But if you don't want to..." he added quickly.

"Nonsense... If it makes you more secure then it will be worth it!"

Pyrra remembered their first flight to Calmor together and the near miss with the glider. Angus slid off her back and nearly ended up in a field near the Irish Sea, having fallen from a couple of thousand feet.

"Let's try it out," she said enthusiastically.

Angus slipped the cracked leather straps round her chest and pulled them tight. The old leather creaked as he pulled and buckled one strap under her front legs and then one higher up around the upper part of her chest.

"We might have to add a new leather strap," he commented, straining with all his might to fasten the buckle.

"Don't be so cheeky young man!" replied Pyrra pretending to be affronted by his remark and sucking her chest in.

Smiling in turn, Angus fastened the buckle and stood back to examine the fit. The seat of the saddle was quite small and did not look designed for comfort. Two loops hung on either side of the lower strap, but unlike stirrups for horse riding, they seemed to be fixed to the leather to just serve as somewhere to hook in your feet. Angus could not see any reins and the only thing to hold onto was a sort of handle in front of the seat, rather like a pommel. He fiddled and pulled the straps as much as he could to get as snug a fit as possible.

"Well get on then!" challenged Pyrra, obviously keen to get going.

Angus grabbed hold of the handle at the front of the saddle and found it much easier to climb on to the dragon's back. The small perch was surprisingly comfortable and somehow reassuring. He had just placed his bum on the saddle when Pyrra flexed her wings in preparation for flight.

"Let's see if it helps you stay on!" said Pyrra mischievously.

No doubt she thought about the remark Angus made about the size of her girth and she jumped, taking off vertically. She barely gave Angus time to secure a foothold. He balanced himself with the aid of the pommel, stretched his legs down felt for the loops with his feet and hooked his trainers into them. Pyrra made for the tree line again and weaved her way in and out of the poplars with great speed and ease. Satisfied that the saddle would indeed help his balance, the pair practised a few more manoeuvres at high speed. Angus hung on for dear life, but enjoyed every minute of the adrenalin buzz as the dragon laid her ears flat, to coax every bit of speed from her body that she possibly could. Pyrra's flying skills had certainly improved over the last few weeks and he could not imagine her ever being quicker than this, even prior to the Great Hibernation.

Afterwards they made their way back to the house and could see Rathlin with Cyru, preparing to tackle the avenue. The blue dragon was tacked up with the ancient saddle and he gave them the 'thumbs up' as he passed. Angus presumed all the other candidates were working hard on their training, and with the time for the Trials drawing near, he was anxious to see Georgina again. They had been emailing each other but her Dad was quite strict about not letting her go off on Godroi without supervision. Not the kind of restriction that parents usually impose on teenagers but none the less just as frustrating!

In the days that followed, Pyrra, with Angus, continued to push her training to the limit. A long flight back to her lair in the mountains being one of the most memorable outings they had. The first, and last, time they visited her hidden cave in the valley, Angus had just became the first member of the SSDP for a long, long time. He stood in the middle of the cave and marvelled at the rocky architecture, once Pyrra had heated up the rock in the centre with her fiery breath. The warm glow from the rock cast an almost sun-like hue over the interior of the cave. Unlike the Cor Stan, this light was orange and cast shadows everywhere; giving the interior a more primal feel. Angus just loved the warmth from the elemental power and was very reluctant to leave the secret lair when Pyrra told him it was time go.

"Don't worry my friend... I will bring you back soon," promised Pyrra as Angus jumped up into the saddle.

"It will have to be before the Trials," he replied dejectedly.

"Why so?" she asked perplexed at his statement.

"Well if you win we won't get another chance… you will have to stay in Krubera and I won't get to see you again!" he managed, only just keeping his emotions in check. The thought of the Trials had excited him at first because of his competitive nature but then he began to realise that winning would mean losing Pyrra and that thought was just something he did not want to consider, such was the bond that they had developed between them.

"I would not have that Angus… you are my protector, yes, but first and foremost my friend. I could not stand to lose you!" she had turned her head to look at him as he sat with his head bowed and giving him a nudge with her nose to look at her, she continued. "I have not dwelled on that thought, as I did not want to think of the consequences either… I do not know what my destiny is but I know that whatever happens, we will always be close and I would find a way to see you, whenever I could" she reassured him.

"Okay," he replied feeling slightly more heartened by this.

On the flight back to Piggleston, Angus tried to put the thought of winning the Trials out of his mind. He knew that Pyrra wanted it, as he did, but the thought of losing her, despite her promise, made him realise that winning would be a bitter sweet victory.

The following Saturday, the Maidens had just come into view and Angus lay almost flat as Pyrra soared downward on her approach to the castle. They had made good time, in fact excellent time. It had only taken just over two hours to fly from home and that was a record for Pyrra. The training was working well and the results were plain to see. She swooped down over the grass and then spreading her wings wide, flicked upright, slowing in an instant and gently touching her back legs down in what was fast becoming her trademark landing. Her Dragonore, and her own senses, told her some other dragons were approaching. Looking towards the lighthouse she could make out Argent with Godroi and hurried off to greet 'the boys'. Angus looked expectantly in the direction the male dragons came from, if the boys were here then surely…

"Hi Angus, looking for me?" whispered Georgina in his ear and making him jump.

"Whoa… I wish you wouldn't do that!" answered Angus, as he spun around to face her, wondering how she always managed to sneak up on him.

"Sorry... did I scare you?" she giggled, flicking her hair out of her face.

"NO..." replied Angus rather too loudly, he tried again but a little more quietly "No, not really... you just surprised me."

Georgina's father, jolly Hugh Penfold, appeared at her back, as usual in his clerical dog collar. Angus' hands felt all clammy and he wiped them on his jeans before offering one to the Vicar.

"Daddy wanted to come up and talk to Rathlin so we brought both the boys..." Georgina smiled at him. "I hoped we'd run into you," she added shyly.

Dermot rustled up something for lunch, always managing no matter how many appeared at the refectory table. As they all ate together it was not long before conversation turned to the Trials and what training the dragons had been doing.

"Cyru has been doing splendidly..." boasted Rathlin, "he may be small in stature but he is stout of heart!" he added proudly.

"Godroi is just a magnificent beast... He is in fine shape and he and Georgina will take some beating, that's for sure," replied Hugh as he turned to Angus, "and what of Pyrra… how is her practise going?"

Angus looked at Hugh and Rathlin in turn. He wanted to tell them that she was so good he was afraid they would have to part with each other forever. He wanted to tell them that, secretly, he hoped she would not give it her best. That deep down, he knew she could win hands, or claws, down.

"She's doing okay… I guess," was all he ended up saying.

"Oh… well I am sure you are just being modest as usual Angus," said Hugh, a little disappointed by the lack of enthusiasm in the reply, as had been looking forward to a lively debate and a bit of verbal jousting.

"Perhaps the dragons could have a little race around the islands. We have some excellent cliffs which would be an ideal test," said Rathlin sensing what the Vicar was after. "Of course we would need to ask the dragons if they were up for the challenge!"

"Indeed!" replied Hugh enthusiastically. "What do you think my boy?"

"Well I don't think Pyrra would like that much…" he replied not very convincingly, "she's a little tired".

"You'll be ready for a race won't you my dear?" said the Vicar trying to use his daughter to bait Angus.

"I'm not so sure Daddy... I would rather stay here," she diplomatically replied, sensing her friend's reluctance, although not knowing his reasons.

"Well let's ask the dragons and then take a vote on it," added Rathlin in a conciliatory tone.

It did not take long for Hugh and Rathlin to persuade Godroi, Argent and Cyru to take part in a race around the tiny group of islands that made up The Maidens. However Pyrra stayed silent throughout the conversation. Angus had rightly guessed and she was not too keen on participating in the test of speed that they had devised. In the end, she only agreed to go after much cajoling from Argent and Godroi.

Soon the four dragons, and their protectors, were lined up on the cliff, just above the hidden entrance to the cavern below Calmor Castle. Dermot stood on the cliff top with a white hankie held above his head. The competitors focused on the grey water beneath and waited for the moment he would drop it and shout, 'GO'. To Angus it seemed like ages before he finally said it, but when he did, all four dragons dived headlong over the edge and down to the grey blue sea stretched below. They all pulled up at the same time and began to turn left towards the other islands. Georgina giggled as she looked across at the row of four dragons flying abreast, and thought 'if they were on horses, it would be a perfect quadrille'. The moment was soon lost as Pyrra almost collided with Argent. He had cut across her path and she just managed to avoid his tail as she deftly rolled sideways. This gave Angus the strangely wonderful view of the sea on his left, the sky on his right and the cliff face where the sky should have been. It took Pyrra four more wing-beats to right herself, as Angus lay flat against her neck and held on as tightly as he could. He glanced at the others and could see that Pyrra had pulled level with Argent, despite initially being blocked by him. Cyru was in front, as he had been furthermost left and therefore got the best start. Godroi, with Georgina, was at the rear but gained fast. They straightened out and headed full pelt to the furthermost island in the small chain. Pyrra sensed Godroi was winning ground so she flattened her ears and stretched her neck increasing her speed.

Angus could see a marker buoy as it floated in the water and its light wink on and off even in the daylight. That was the point they had agreed they would switch into dragon time. He watched as Pyrra reached it at the same time as Godroi and Cyru. All three were now neck and neck. The dragons used their magical ability to slow down the world around them. Behind them Argent, who was not in the Trials and therefore had not trained as hard as the others, struggled to keep up; especially with the disadvantage of carrying the portly Vicar.

The thrashing tide beneath them instantly slowed down, the waves seemingly hung in the air and the salty spray floated off the crests. Angus could see the light on the buoy flash more slowly and felt the thrill and exhilaration he always did when they moved up a gear into the dragon's highest speed. He looked across at the others and could see that they were blurring in and out of focus. He had not witnessed another dragon in dragon time before and he surmised that the distortion was due to the fact that they were not all going at exactly the same speed. Pyrra started to bank left and he turned to see that they had already reached the outermost island and had now turned back in the direction of Calmor. Godroi started to pull ahead but Angus knew that Pyrra could go faster than this. He realised Georgina was watching and she grinned at him from her perch on Godroi's back, lying low like Angus to help streamline as much as possible. He smiled back and began to encourage Pyrra in answer to the silent challenge from Georgina.

"C'mon Pyrra, we can take them!" he shouted.

Pyrra responded by stretching her neck further and she increased the rhythm of her beating wings. Angus grinned and pinned himself to her neck as he shouted more words of encouragement. They swept past the north of Calmor Island and headed towards the other little islands. He risked a backwards glance and could see that Cyru had fallen behind with Argent was a long way back. It was not long before they had made the last turn and began the final straight, racing back to Calmor. Angus could see the lighthouse as they fast approached the tall white tower. It was at that point that they had agreed to complete the race through the cliffs.

Both Pyrra and Godroi rounded the lighthouse and dropped down to the rocks, coming very close to hitting each other. Pyrra just managed to get in front as they reached a split in the rock faces and forced Godroi to fall in behind them. Angus glanced back to see that Godroi was all over them, trying to find a way past Pyrra in the tight space between the main island and the pillars of rock that had been formed through thousands of years of storm erosion. He looked on as Pyrra ploughed into a flock of seagulls, static in mid-flight and directly in her path. The birds bounced off her body and wings and Angus wondered if they would even realise that something had hit them. He could see that they appeared frozen in position, wings spread as they rolled past her body in a slow motion tumble.

An archway in the rock appeared suddenly as they turned the next bend. Pyrra decided to dive for the gap but had to fold her wings back to squeeze through. This forced her to slow down before she could unfold her wings and start beating to increase her speed again. Godroi had flown over the archway and his speed brought him in front of Pyrra much to the delight of Georgina who squealed support from behind his golden head. Angus bellowed his own support to Pyrra, egging her on. He knew there would be no living with Godroi if he won. The golden dragon had two females to impress and no Argent to rival him, since he had fallen way behind with Cyru. Godroi decided to step up the pace a little and started to perform some aerobatics trying to show off his flying skills. Angus watched as he flipped into a barrel roll narrowly missing the cliff edge. His antics did not have the desired affect as Georgina had a hard job hanging on to him. One of her hands lost grip and her arm flailed around, almost unseating her. Pyrra sped up alongside Godroi and growled something in his direction. From the look on his face she had not paid him a compliment and he ducked his head down, driving onwards towards the finish line, which was the top of the cliff at the castle.

They cleared the rocky walls and began to race across the bay, Godroi edged just ahead of Pyrra by keeping himself low over the water. Pyrra was much higher at this point and as the cliff loomed in front of her Angus could see that they would make it to the top easily. Godroi had decided to skim the waves with his legs and had left his ascent to the last second. The golden dragon raised his head and aimed for the top of the cliff but as he reached it he tried to flatten out far too quickly and clipped the edge on his way past. Angus watched helplessly as Godroi flipped and spun out of control just as he and Pyrra passed over them. The final outcome was hidden from their view.

What Angus missed, was Georgina's flip from Godroi's back as he somersaulted tail over head to land unceremoniously on his back. He continued to roll over until he hit the side of the castle. By the time Pyrra had switched back to normal time and returned to Godroi, he was already sitting up as he rubbed his head groggily.

"You great oaf Godroi, are you alright?" she chided.

"Ugh… what… yes I'm fine…"

"Where's Georgina?" shouted Angus.

Angus started to call out her name and ran to the edge of the cliff, but could see no sign of her. He was nearly bowled over by Cyru as he flew past.

Godroi and Pyrra joined in the search and that was when Angus noticed the large patch of Blue Dragon Fire, some metres away, giving off its pungent aniseed smell as if it had been disturbed. He ran over and at first he could not see anything. Angus was about to give up when he heard a groan coming from under the plants and pulled the fragrant blue flowers aside to find Georgina. Soon she was sitting on the grass covered cliff top rubbing her head, hair falling over her face and more shaken than hurt.

Godroi went into one of his flowery profuse apologies and did the dragon equivalent of a bow. Georgina started laughing at once as she could not be cross with him for long, but her father could. He had just arrived to hear what had happened and he fumed and raged at Godroi, who hung his head low in abject apology.

"I'm fine Daddy…" she said intervening and saving Godroi from a further tongue lashing by the Vicar.

She patted the subdued dragon on the nose and noticed a patch of his jewels were missing from his lower chest.

"Godroi what happened to your chest?" she asked concerned.

"Oh, nothing to worry about… they must have come off during my little mishap," he deflected, pleased that his young protector was not physically hurt and thinking it was just as well her father had not seen what had happened or he may have stopped them flying together in the future!

"Not to worry Godroi…" said Cyru with a smirk, "at least you don't have to worry about any knights looking to lance you nowadays!"

"Yes and hopefully Godroi has learned his lesson and will curb his enthusiasm for over zealous manoeuvres… at least until the Trials," added Pyrra disapprovingly.

## Chapter 14

## *'Fire and Faith'*

With school finished Angus and Pyrra increased their training schedule until the lad felt he knew what the dragon was going to do, before she actually did it. Soon the companions found themselves standing in the cavern under Calmor Castle. Once again they waited with the rest of the challengers to find out what was to happen next.

Miss Puttick, now Mrs Tek, had paid Angus' parents a visit to ask if he could come to Calmor for a holiday, thus clearing the way for them to go to Krubera. Georgina and Angus caught up with each others news about everything from school to how well the training was going. It was during this conversation that Fergus sidled over to them with Felspar at his side. Angus waited on another smart and condescending comment from one of them, but what was said surprised both him and Pyrra.

"Hi Georgina… Angus… Listen I think I owe you an apology…" said Fergus without looking Angus in the eye, "I was out of order last time we met and to be honest… a little jealous of you."

"You! Jealous of me?" replied Angus disbelievingly, "No way!"

"Well you did all that stuff for the SSDP and I thought that maybe you would be full of your own self importance..." he looked at Angus with a weak smile on his face, "well... anyway... sorry" he finished, holding out his hand for Angus to shake.

Georgina grinned in obvious pleasure at Fergus' change in attitude towards her friend. Encouraged by this he shook Fergus by the hand and accepted his apology.

They talked animatedly about the Trials and the training they had undertaken since The Gathering. A lot of friendly banter rang round the secret cavern, which belied the serious rivalry between the competitors. Felspar stood behind them and watched, saying nothing. He was a dragon of very few words and preferred to keep his own counsel. Pyrra kept an eye on the black dragon for a while and wondered why he was not as boastful as he had been on the day of the choosing. She simply put it down to high spirits at that time. Despite her best efforts to introduce herself and be friendly she was most put out that the black dragon make no effort at all to speak to her, or indeed any of them. In fact Pyrra found he decidedly lacked any social graces and was rather ignorant. She was still prepared to think he might be nervous about the task in hand.

After a while Rathlin called for silence. At long last it was time for the ten contenders, with their protectors, to listen to the final briefing, before the contest began in earnest. Everyone gathered around him to listen to the instructions he had to give and Angus moved forward to get a better view.

"Move aside!" growled Macklin, the fiery red dragon, as he physically pushed Angus aside and took his place in the circle. The young lad glanced up at the angry beast and remembered how his temper had been all too evident during the choosing ceremony. Macklin's protector was Chad a surly American boy who just glared at Angus, as if sizing up an enemy. Angus decided to ignore them, instead moving to stand beside Fergus and Georgina. The speech that followed was relatively short; all of the contestants were to follow Pyrra and Cyru to the clearing at the Krubera cave entrance. It was from there that they would be given further instructions. The Trials could then be started and events ultimately deciding, who the next Ward should be, would take place.

Seven hours later, the last of the ten dragons touched down in the clearing on the windswept and desolate mountainside that rose above the Krubera caves. The competitors stood around looking at the harsh surroundings they now found themselves in and Angus took comfort from the fact that at least Rathlin and he had a slight advantage. They had been here before. Each of the ten protectors had a backpack, sleeping bag, cooking stove, utensils and some provisions that Rathlin had suggested they bring. Like a Scoutmaster going on a camping trip, he had sensibly put together an inventory and a brief outline of what to expect. Pyrra nudged Angus and he turned to see that The Watcher, elusive and mysterious as ever, waited for them at the entrance.

"Follow me," called a voice from the depths of his hood, and directing them inside the entrance, he disappeared from sight.

Everyone stood and looked at each other until Rathlin nodded at Angus and cocked his head towards the entrance with a wink. The others, led by the head of the SSDP, followed Angus in and were guided down to the magical wall that cloaked the corridor beyond. As each dragon and protector passed through the wall, Angus listened to the gasps of surprise and looks of awe, greatly amused by their reactions. When they arrived at the mirror cavern Georgina squealed with delight at the beautiful scene that met the competitors. In total contrast to everyone else, being totally focused on the competition, Godroi was not quite as chatty as he usually was. In truth he was anxious to meet Ward Barfoot and have the first task explained to him.

He did not have to wait long because as they filtered further into the mirror cavern they gradually, one by one, became aware that they were already in the presence of the spectral dragon and a hush went round like an echo. Barfoot stood majestically in the centre of the large cavern and waited patiently for everyone to recover from the splendid sight around them. Dragons and protectors stared silently captivated by the ghostly opaque form that had seemingly materialised from thin air.

"Greetings freonds welcome to Krubera ham of the Cor Stan…" he lifted his front claw and swept it in the direction of the cavern beyond, "I am Ward Barfoot and I am most delighted to greet you all."

At that Godroi stepped forward and introduced himself, with the other dragons following his cue.

"Ah Pyrra, I am very pleased to see that you have been chosen to take part," he said, nodding his head to her, "and indeed, you too Cyru. May good fortune grace you both and all worthy competitors," he finished.

Barfoot then introduced himself to the awestruck protectors, taking his time to greet every single one of them by name and leaving Angus and Rathlin to last. The formalities complete, they followed him to the end of the cavern and through the tunnels until they came to the place that Pyrra and Angus had explored on their last visit, some months previously. Each dragon and their protector were allocated one of the caves that would provide a temporary home during the Trials.

"Please get a good night's rest and tomorrow I will explain the first task," said Barfoot before he departed to his own cave.

Everyone immediately began to talk about Barfoot and all they had seen. No-one noticed the shrouded figure standing in a darkened entrance, soundlessly living up to his name and watching their every move until every human and dragon drifted off to sleep.

No-one could tell whether it was morning or not from inside the cave and despite being constantly bathed in the pale blue light the protectors stirred, one by one, replete with sleep. They got up and washed in a natural spring that ran through one end of the cavern, spraying a fountain of freezing white water into the air as it forced its way through the rock wall. Angus, and a few of the others, went through the embarrassing routine of finding out how the toilet facilities worked. The same stream of water forced its way into a smaller cave beyond and from there it disappeared downwards into a natural whirlpool. Angus burst out laughing when he heard Georgina announce, very indignantly, that she would not be going to the toilet for a week. He found it all very fascinating, but it was not something many people were comfortable with and a system was devised to allow protectors their privacy, whenever they plucked up the courage to use the amenities. Needless to say, no-one used it much on the first day.

Soon they had all eaten and The Watcher made it known that it was time, once more, to follow him. He led them to yet another cave and left Angus wondering just how vast the system really was. Barfoot stood waiting to address the assembly and Angus realised, he was actually quite nervous now. He looked at Georgina and could see that she was too, but he drew strength from the fact that Pyrra seemed quite calm. Her ears were flattened down close to her head, which Angus knew to mean she had totally focused her energies and shutting everything else out of her mind. Her breathing was slow and rhythmic, and that gave him immense comfort.

Ward Barfoot greeted the contenders and began to explain the first task.

"Good morning…" he said as he surveyed the faces before him, smiling at each, and somehow putting them at ease, "I hope you slept well my freonds?" A few heads nodded and a couple of nervously mumbled replies answered him. This gave Angus the impression of a

Headmaster, addressing a class of children who were not quite sure if they were in trouble or not.

"At last it is time to start the Trials and your first task will be to walk through the cave behind me and into the next cavern… I will be waiting for you all and only those with absolute trust and faith in each other will be able to proceed." He scanned the faces again as if to reassure them that everything would be okay, but Angus could not foresee any great difficulty about passing through the cave that Barfoot had mentioned. "The Watcher will let you know when your time is at hand."

With that said, the Ward turned and walked into the cave behind him. As he did so, flames engulfed the entrance and produced gasps of horror from all of the protectors. The fire began to follow him until no-one could make out anything beyond the raging inferno they now realised they had to pass through. The dragons stood motionless and the protectors shuffled nervously as The Watcher walked towards Macklin and Chad, pointed to them and then gestured towards the flames. Chad climbed onto the back of the red beast and held on tight, sweat beginning to dimple his forehead. Macklin stepped forward and growled something to the boy, then entered the flames.

Everyone held their breath as the fire engulfed the two and eventually veiled them from sight. Angus watched as three more protectors went through, one after the other, all apprehensively sitting atop a dragon. Angus realised that their turn would surely be coming soon. He knew that Pyrra would be fine, as her scales would protect her from the fiercest heat or fire, but he would be decidedly more vulnerable to the flames. This would be a true test of nerves. He looked on as The Watcher pointed to Godroi and Georgina. She climbed nervously up onto his golden back and closed her eyes tightly. The girl clung to his back as he walked through the flames. The next pairing were nominated by the silent hooded figure and Angus realised that it was their turn now. He desperately did not want to let Pyrra down, but he shook with fear and hoped that no-one would notice. Pyrra could feel him trembling as he lay tightly to her back. She turned to him just before she moved into the flames.

"Close your eyes Angus and trust me, you will not get burned," she calmly assured him. He did as he was told and closed his eyes. "Now concentrate on me and clear your mind of thoughts and fears. Can you feel my mind reaching out to you?" she whispered to him encouragingly.

At first he could not sense anything, but then his mind began to feel a tendril of thought that was not his own. He latched onto it and then more of them came, assuaging his senses. They were not real thoughts as such, but more sensations of colour, smell, and something else Angus could not describe, however he did understand what they meant.

"Yes!" replied Angus incredulously.

He put everything else out of his mind he concentrated on Pyrra and what she was feeling. She transmitted thoughts of serenity, calm and well being; before, slowly and carefully, she walked through the flames. Angus could not see the flames but he was no longer afraid, now that his mind was connected to Pyrra's. He braced himself as she

began to walk forward. In his ears he could hear the flames crackle and flicker around him as Pyrra strode, on and on, further into the inferno. It took him a few seconds to realise that the fire was not burning him. Instead his skin felt as if cold lizard tongues were licking it. Disbelieving his sense of touch he opened his eyes and instinctively raised his hands to his face to protect himself from the engulfing flames that surrounded his body.

"Keep your eyes closed Angus or your mind will believe it is being burned and you will feel the pain even though nothing is burning you!" called Pyrra loudly over the roaring noise.

He did as he was told and quickly found the connection with her mind again. Once again he began to enjoy the chilled sensation he felt from then on.

"You can open your eyes now Angus," said Barfoot. They had passed through the fiery curtain and Angus looked back to see that the flames still blazed as fiercely as they had appeared from the other side. "Well done both of you… if you can please join the others," said Barfoot, pointing to the other end of the grotto they now found themselves in.

They both went to join Godroi and Georgina to congratulate them.

"Thanks," said Georgina, "I knew you wouldn't have any trouble Angus!"

"You're joking! I was totally scared," he replied honestly. "If it wasn't for Pyrra I would have never have got through!"

"To be honest I was the same until Godroi spoke to me," she said as she reached up and patted Godroi affectionately on his side.

They turned to watch as Cyru emerged from the flames carrying a ghostly Rathlin completely chalk white as the colour had drained from his normally ruddy cheeks. It took him a few minutes before he recovered enough to speak and, even then, he could not complete a full sentence. Eventually nine dragons and their protectors stood in front of Barfoot, the flames died away and The Watcher walked through the cave to take his familiar place at the Ward's side. They had a short whispered conversation and then Barfoot spoke.

"Very well…" he said before he turned to face them. "I am sorry to say that Gilmor will not be joining us…" Barfoot looked genuinely saddened, "Unfortunately he, and his young protector Liam, will not be able to continue in the

Trials… but they have another important task to do for me and I know I can trust them to see it through."

Angus was still stunned that he had managed to overcome his own fear and felt no heat when they passed through the flames. He had checked and touched his clothes many times expecting them to be scorched and he was amazed to find they felt quite cold for several minutes afterwards. Pyrra had just smiled at him wisely and explained that it was because of his total trust in her that they managed to come through the first challenge unscathed.

"You have had a hard few hours in this first test and you will all need to get a good nights rest, as the next test will be harder…" continued Ward Barfoot gravely, "but I must congratulate you all as you have shown that you already have some of the qualities required to continue in your quest!" he said with immense pleasure.

## Chapter 15

# 'Victory and Misfortune'

Although the dragons and protectors had not exerted themselves much in the way of physical exercise during the first task, mentally, they were all exhausted as they trudged wearily back to their caves to rest. They arrived to find Gilmor was still there with Liam, obviously very upset.

"I think we should go and speak to him Angus," said Georgina as some of the dragons commiserated with Gilmor.

"Yeah I guess," replied Angus, not comfortable with this kind of situation.

He recalled talking to Liam on the night of The Gathering; the lad was the same age as Angus, with short, spiked, reddish hair and enjoyed telling jokes. They both walked over and sat beside Liam, who had obviously been crying but was trying hard to hide it as everyone else came back.

"Hi Liam… how are you?" asked Georgina tentatively.

"Oh I'll be fine… but I've really let Gilmor down," he sniffed.

"I am sure he won't blame you…" she assured, "don't you agree Angus?"

"Eh... oh... well of course he won't," replied Angus unconvincingly.

Georgina frowned at him willing him to be a bit more supportive. Angus tried again.

"You know I nearly didn't go through the flames either!" he added trying to make up for his poor first attempt at sympathy.

"Na way... for sure you're just saying tha to make me feel better" replied Liam disbelievingly in his broad Irish accent.

"No honestly... ask Pyrra... I was really scared until she talked me into it," added Angus, "If it wasn't for her I would be going home with you!"

"Godroi did the same for me too!" said Georgina.

"Well I just couldn't believe Gilmor when he said I would be okay with my eyes shut... but thanks for making me realise I wasn't the only one having trouble, for sure I really appreciate it," said Liam smiling for the first time since they had returned from to the cave.

"So what will you do now?" asked Georgina.

"Well first I'll be heading back to Calmor on a little errand for Ward Barfoot and then I'll go home to Dublin." he answered.

"Will you be alright on your own?" asked Georgina, concerned.

"Ah sure I will… Gilmor knows the way," he winked.

"What did Barfoot ask you to do?" probed Angus.

"Now that'd be telling, wouldn't it?" replied Liam with a smile, "and if I did tha, I'd hav'ta shoot ya!"

They all laughed at his joke and talked until it was time for Gilmor and him to go, only stopping to say goodbye to Farrel before they left.

Angus lay, restless in his sleeping bag, replaying the events of that day through his head, again and again.

"Pyrra are you asleep?" he whispered into the darkness.

"How can I with you making so much noise with your thoughts," she said jovially.

"I was just wondering what you did today?" he asked.

"It's hard to explain…" she paused as if unable to answer, "but basically, I connected my mind to yours."

"I didn't know you could do that!"

"It's an old skill and I wasn't sure we could do it, but it was the only thing I could think of and I have always sensed you and I had a connection," explained Pyrra.

"Did the others do the same?"

"More or less..." she sighed heavily, "Although Liam could not connect well enough with Gilmor to allow them to complete the task."

"But how did you do it?" probed Angus, eager to find out more.

"It involves a subconscious link between my mind and yours," she explained, "and it can only exist between two minds that are completely open to each other."

"Can you tell what I am thinking?" asked Angus.

"Not really... At least not yet anyway!" she laughed. "It's more like being able to pick up your feelings. If we keep at it, we will be able to do a lot more and I suspect we might need to for some of the Trials" she finished sagely.

"I know what you mean. I have sensed your moods and feelings before," said Angus, thinking about what she had just said, "I only just realised that now though."

"That's interesting..." he could not see her thoughtful expression in the dark, "We shall have to work on it, but I have heard that long ago, it was possible to read thoughts once the link was strong enough."

Angus went off to sleep thinking about reading Pyrra's mind and when he awoke the next morning he recalled the strangest dream about a dragon he was sure he had never met before. He quickly put it out of his mind and went off to wash, and the toilet facilities had to be tackled as a matter of urgency!

Soon the nine remaining teams were ready and all eagerly awaited the next task to be explained by Ward Barfoot.

"Congratulations once again to you who have managed to come through the curtain of fire. Your next Trial awaits you and this will test your flying skill, as well as your nerves," said the commanding voice of the Ward. "Soon you will all be taken to a vast chamber but before that each dragon must be blindfolded and their protector gagged." The assembled contestants started to murmur and fidget at the last statement.

"Do not be overly concerned my freonds," he went on, "The chamber is filled with pillars that rise from the floor to the ceiling. Your task is to navigate to the other end where, once again, I will be waiting for you," continued Barfoot. "The protectors will be immobilised so that he, or she, can neither use arms nor legs to influence the dragon's steering. You must not touch any other dragon or any part of the cave..."

'This is going to be very tricky indeed', Angus thought and hoped Pyrra could not read his mind. He was glad they had put in all those hours of practice, especially the sessions flying around the mountains at Pyrra's cave. The swooping and weaving in and out of the tree-lined avenue at Long Reach would also come in handy. He could see Rathlin grinning at him, obviously thinking the same thing.

"The Watcher will show you where to start this next Trial. I wish you all good fortune and look forward to seeing you afterwards," said Barfoot before turning and passing through an opening behind him.

The ever-present Watcher led the nine pairs of anxious contestants into an ante-room and explained again that beyond the next passageway lay a huge cathedral-like cavern.

"You will be split into three heats and I will lead each heat through," he instructed.

Angus felt that The Watcher appeared to stare at Rathlin for a few seconds, as the head of the SSDP tried to rouse some enthusiasm from Cyru. At least the dark hood faced in Rathlin's direction as no features could be seen within it.

"Once we enter the arena, you will not be allowed to speak... Any questions?" he finished, the darkened hole turning to scan the room. "Good, let's go!"

As The Watcher split them into three groups, Georgina squeezed Angus' arm and whispered 'good luck'.

"What do you reckon?" he asked Pyrra softly so as not to be overheard.

"No problem... I thought it would be something like this. I will be relying solely on you to get through this Trial and you must have absolute faith in me, just as before. Do not be afraid, just think of it as another practise up at Long Reach, in and out of the trees," she winked at him then added. "You know I won't let anything happen to you, so don't worry. You will be able to see the obstacles coming and you must concentrate fully on them and nothing else... I will be using your eyes... Do you understand?"

Angus patted her neck in response and felt at ease. He wondered if he would feel anything, however his thoughts were interrupted as hoods and gags were prepared for the first group.

Godroi was led through, closely followed by Farrel and Leofric, into the big cave and with their respective protectors saddled above them. The protectors were not only gagged but their saddles had been padded at the legs to stop them being able to steer, in jockey fashion, with nudges. Both hands were strapped to the handles of the new saddles, which were made for each contestant courtesy of Rathlin. Only he and Angus had the original Tek saddles, found in the attic at Long Reach. Georgina sat on Godroi's back, shaking, as she surveyed the vast cavern before her with its multitude of haphazard pillars strewn between them and Barfoot. The Ward stood some two hundred metres away across the cavern floor strewn with boulders of many sizes. She could see places where the ceiling had caved in or stalactites hung menacingly in the paths they would have to take. Watery channels ran through the cavern in many places, adding to the feeling that this cave was in a perpetual state of transformation and would probably be different every time you came back. The three dragons were lined up by The Watcher and told to be ready for the signal. Georgina looked to her left and could see that Halla, and the gagged Peter, looked nervous as well.

"Concentrate on the pillars!" said the muffled voice of Godroi from under his hood. He risked breaking the rules in an effort to calm his protector. Just as she did so, Georgina suddenly felt her brooch glow fiercely and Godroi spread his wings to lift them off the ground. He moved forward at a steady pace, sensible in these treacherous conditions and she was glad that he showed more restraint, than he had during the race at Calmor. She concentrated on the pillars in front of them and resisted the temptation to look in any other direction but forward. Knowing that their success relied on her ability to focus on the task in hand was not easy to deal with and she found it hard enough not to blink. The first pillar loomed and all other thoughts were purged from her mind as Godroi sought the link with her mind!

Angus sat motionless as the next three pairings were led through. The waiting was agonising and he began to wonder if he could open his mind enough for Pyrra to get in. Then he felt the same sensation he had the day before, during the first trial. At first, he felt as though he imagined it, but then he knew that he could sense Pyrra and he latched onto her mind with all his will.

"That's good Angus... Keep me in your mind and we will get through this easily," she said confidently through the hood.

He was so focused on keeping her link with him, he had not been aware of the time, and was surprised when The

Watcher motioned them forward and positioned them in the cavern beyond. Angus marvelled at the scene before him and took in the detail of every pillar within his field of vision. The rock columns gave the cavern a labyrinth-like feel.

Through his mind, Pyrra could make up a mental picture of the obstacles before her and was able to plot the path she wanted. To her it was not like true vision but more like a strangely coloured sonar scan. She began to concentrate on the path she felt was best and transmitted calming thoughts to her young protector. Angus felt his Dragonore heat up against his chest and leaned forward as Pyrra lifted off and headed in the direction she had planned using his eyes. His mouth was dry, but there was no going back now. Angus could do nothing but sit quietly, emptying his thoughts and concentrate on the pillars they had to avoid.

As Pyrra started flying, he could sense all the tension leave his body and he felt at one with the green dragon. Immediately she flew straight between the two nearest pillars and turned left around another, close to the edge of the cavern. Angus concentrated his whole mind to take in the darkened interior and as obstacles loomed, he thought hard about the necessary evasive action. Pyrra responded to his mind signals with ease, the pair were so in tune with each other they could have been one being. He marvelled at her grace as she weaved her way, easily past, each subsequent column that presented itself as a possible danger. Soon Barfoot was very near and Pyrra negotiated the last obstacle to land deftly in front of the great dragon.

"Well done Pyrra... You may remove your hood," he called to her.

As she did so, Angus felt the link between them sever, as if someone had physically cut the invisible strand. He turned to see Nehebkau coming in to land just next them. However, his attention was drawn back to the pillars as Leofric's flight seemed to get more and more erratic. Angus watched helplessly as the dragon's right wingtip collided with a large column and caused the dragon to spin out of control. Leofric's wings folded up as he crashed to the ground in an ungainly heap and almost rolled over onto his protector Halla, who, against all expectation, had somehow managed to stay on the dragon's back throughout the whole drama. By the time the others reached them, Halla had managed to free herself and was in tears while she hugged Leofric around his brown neck. Barfoot quickly made sure that both were okay and apart from Leofric's pride, a sore neck and a scraped wing, they both assured the anxious crowd that they were fine.

Soon they were back with the others and Angus was very pleased to see that Georgina smiled happily and obviously still in one piece.

"Oh Angus, tell me you got through okay?" she pleaded.

"Of course we did," he winked, "What about you two?"

"Of course we did!" she replied, mimicking him, "But it was terrible, poor Oswin and Farrel collided with each other almost immediately!" she exclaimed.

"NO WAY!" he said a bit more loudly than he intended, "Leofric clipped a wing as well... What about the others?" he continued, a little more quietly.

"Rathlin's heat all got through, so that leaves just six of us left now," she answered waving over towards Rathlin. Oswin and Leofric talked animatedly in a corner as Lars hugged his distraught sister, Halla, beside them. Angus spotted Kadin with Fergus and decided to go over to congratulate them on winning through the challenge. Both he and the others praised or commiserated each of the protectors in turn, until finally, he reached Rathlin and was given a hearty handshake by the pony-tailed leader of the SSDP.

"Angus… well done. Pyrra tells me you did a great job," he enthused.

"We make a good team but she did most of the work," replied Angus modestly.

"Nonsense, she told me you could not have done better and I nearly blew our chances," he divulged.

"Really… How come?" asked a surprised Angus.

"Well I lost my cool a little when that fool Macklin forced his way in front of us…" he shot an angry glance over at the red dragon, "He almost pushed us into the side wall, but fortunately Cyru managed to avoid hitting anything with some brilliant flying," he said as he clapped his hand proudly on the back of the young blue dragon.

"Did they apologise?" asked Angus, as he glanced at the angry Macklin.

"No they did not... but I gave them a piece of my mind that's for sure!" shouted Rathlin loudly, drawing the growling attentions of Chad and Macklin in their direction. Angus could not help but notice that they stared at Rathlin for some time after that and his dislike of the pair grew more when he heard them boast about how they had nearly forced Cyru into the cavern wall.

Barfoot announced that it was now time to return back to the living quarters, but he told them that they were free to come and go to the surface as they pleased, as long as they did not draw attention to the entrance. Pleased to be free from the constraints of the hood, Pyrra was ecstatic about their success, and delighted with her young protector's performance. She felt they were in perfect harmony with each other now and could achieve much more than they had to date. The nine dragons and humans followed Barfoot through the system of caves. Angus looked up ahead and could see that he and Pyrra were almost last, with Cyru and Rathlin just behind. Just in front of him, Halla and Lars talked with Georgina and he was glad to see that Chad and Macklin some distance away, being nearly at the exit of the tunnel they were in. It was there that The Watcher waited in typically ominous fashion and only moved off, as Felspar passed him. Angus was then distracted from his study of the others by Rathlin, who tapped him on the shoulder.

"Do you fancy going up for some fresh air?" he asked. Pyrra and Angus nodded their agreement. They had all but cleared the long passageway. Only Cyru lagged wearily behind exhausted from his exertions.

"So what do you think of the ancient saddle now then?" ribbed Rathlin.

Despite his earlier derogatory comments, Angus had to admit it was an extremely handy thing to have, considering the flying manoeuvres they had just completed. He admitted as much to Rathlin and offered a tongue in cheek apology. Rathlin laughed and clapped him on the back and just as they left the tunnel, the head of the SSDP started to turn back towards Cyru. At that precise moment a noise like thunder echoed in the caves. The passageway caved in and covered everything in rocks, debris and dust. Angus was sprayed by a few small stones but dodged most of it as he ducked behind Pyrra's body. The others rushed back to see what had happened and as the dust settled it became apparent that Rathlin and Cyru had been caught in the cave-in. The head of the SSDP was at the edge of the tunnel and picked himself up as they reached him. Although, not badly hurt, he was quite shocked and struggled to his feet more concerned for poor Cyru who had taken the brunt of the rock fall. By the time they managed to dig the young blue dragon free it was clear he would not be able to fly too far. His right wing was badly damaged.

"How long will it take to mend?" asked Lars.

"Too long for the Trials, I fear," lamented Oswin. Rathlin was unhappy about Cyru's injury and Barfoot explained that although cave-ins were commonplace, the tunnels they would be using had all been shored up for safety.

"I'm afraid we will have to withdraw from the Trials," said a dejected Rathlin.

"No Rathlin… I will be fine…" interrupted Cyru, anxious not to let Rathlin down by an enforced exit from the competition. "Look I can still move my wing… AARRGH!" he growled as he flexed it unsuccessfully.

"I am sorry for you both and looking at the rocks above, it seems that a wedge has been removed, weakening the roof," said Barfoot sadly.

A heated discussion broke out in light of this observation and Angus looked around for the ever present hooded figure. Sure enough he spotted him lurking in the background and as usual, amidst the uproar, he was noticeable by his silence. Angus began to have his suspicions about the secretive figure and wondered if he were somehow responsible for triggering the cave-in.

## Chapter 16

# *'Reveal-ations'*

As soon as they returned to the sleeping quarters Angus called Georgina to one side and told her of his suspicions about The Watcher.

"But why would he do that?" she asked, shocked at the suggestion.

"I don't know but I'm going to find out and hopefully you and Rathlin will be willing to help me," he said.

"I'm not sure Angus. You have no proof… and what if you are wrong?"

"I'm sure it was him, I saw him lurking at that very spot just before it happened and I've seen him staring at Rathlin all the time… I know he is up to something!" he replied fervently.

Rathlin soon came back having made sure that Cyru was comfortable and listened intently to Angus' theories.

"So you think he's trying to eliminate dragons from the competition unfairly, but what on earth would his motive be?" he asked, having the same doubts as Georgina.

"I don't know, but I really think we should ask him…" replied Angus, "Trouble is he never seems to leave Barfoot's side!"

It was true The Watcher always hung around Ward Barfoot so Georgina, Rathlin and Angus decided that if they were going to confront him, they would need to make sure that Barfoot was not around. Georgina offered to distract the Ward whilst Angus and Rathlin cornered The Watcher in an attempt to get the truth out of him. They agreed to wait until after dinner, so Angus went about the task of preparing and eating his food, all the while trying to figure out what it was about the hooded man he did not trust.

A few strange things had happened to him recently, starting with the dream about Barfoot, the strange one last night about a dragon he had never ever seen before, and the fact that Barfoot seemed to know him. 'That was it!' thought Angus. He had just realised 'Barfoot knew about the SSDP!' As Angus pieced it together, he realised the only way to confirm his suspicions, was to get The Watcher on his own. He dared not say anything to Rathlin yet, at least until he was sure about his theories. He finished his dinner as quickly as he could and coerced Rathlin into going through with the scheme.

The pair walked with Georgina to Barfoot's cave. She tentatively approached his stately figure and told him she needed to speak to him alone. As they had hoped, Barfoot dismissed The Watcher to allow her privacy and they followed him from The Ward's lair. They worried that he would see them and stayed as far away as they could, just in case their Dragonore gave them away. They managed to follow him until he reached his own quarters, which turned out to be hidden away in a deserted part of the

vast caverns. They waited for several minutes trying to work out the best way to approach him. The cave he had entered was hidden by a combination of wood and cloths which shrouded the interior. They decided to hide their precious Dragonore under a rock allowing them to cautiously approach the cave undetected. Angus peered in and could see that the mysterious figure had removed his hood, but had his back to them so this did not allow him to confirm his suspicions. Rathlin bravely moved closer and without further ado, strode into the cave.

"Now sir… We'd like a word!" he shouted, spinning The Watcher around to face him, "What the… strike a light! B… but how on earth!"

Finian Tek stood before Rathlin, who was so stunned he had to sit down on the cave floor before his legs gave way. Angus had got it right! It took Rathlin a few minutes before he recovered from the shock of seeing his dead brother alive and well, standing before him. Angus still could not believe he had guessed correctly, even when the evidence was there in front of his own eyes. Finian courteously asked them to have a seat and poured some water for Rathlin to sip while he recovered from the shock of having his late brother come back to life.

"So you knew who I was all along?" Finian asked, after Angus had explained how he had surmised the truth.

"Not really… I only worked it out this afternoon," replied Angus, with Rathlin looking on like a man who had seen a ghost.

"But what have you been doing for the last three years? Everyone thinks you're dead!" managed Rathlin eventually.

"Well, as Angus had discovered, I was originally looking for the Cor Stan and all my studies had finally led me here…" he said and gestured towards the caves in general, "After I failed to persuade you to join me in the family business, I decided to try and find the Cor Stan on my own."

"And then you found it, and Barfoot?" added Angus.

"Good Lord no… I had to search many cave systems before I found Krubera," replied Finian. "It took me about fourteen years of endless caving to finally get to this location. The only thing I knew was that it was high in the mountains of this region."

"So you'd been searching all that time?" enquired Angus truly impressed.

"Not quite, I was trying to look after as many of the dragons as I could, and find protectors at the same time," answered Finian, "When I first came to Krubera, I had one of the local guides with me, as was normal… we entered the cave system at another point further down the mountain and began to make our way slowly through the caves," he grimaced at the memory, "It was hard going, as some of the tunnels were scarcely big enough to crawl through."

"What happened next?" asked Angus sitting on the edge of his seat.

"The cave roof fell in on me!" replied Finian, obviously not relishing the memories he now had to relive.

"What about the guide?" pushed Angus.

"As far as I could tell, he was unhurt. The rocks had missed him and I could hear him calling me, but I could not answer, so he left to get help..." he held his hand up and pointed to a great scar on his head, partially hidden by his long straggly grey hair, "I must have lay there for days and when I finally regained consciousness long enough, I could see that I had dropped through the floor of the cave and into another system... this one!"

"So Ward Barfoot found you then?" asked Rathlin.

"No I found him... you see, I was badly injured and I lost my Dragonore in the accident so the only thing I could do was crawl in the direction of the strange blue light that seemed to be coming from within the caves," he paused and drank some more water. "The light you see now is much brighter than before and after gathering all my remaining strength, I dragged myself towards the light source... It took me a long time, but I finally found the object of my journey... the Cor Stan!"

"Awesome!" exclaimed Angus, loving every bit of his story.

"I picked up a shard of the great stone, recognising it for what it was and in doing so Barfoot was revealed to me as he lay sleeping next to The Cor Stan."

"So how have you managed to survive all this time?" asked an incredulous Rathlin.

"With Barfoot's help and the power of the Cor Stan, my strength slowly returned, allowing me to venture out and get the supplies I needed... at first I stayed because I was still too weak to return home and then I learned that my demise had been assumed after the guide returned with help and could not find me... I seized the chance to stay and recover fully, whilst helping Barfoot to restore the caves in preparation for the return of all dragons and thus fulfilling my dream," he replied, as Rathlin finished off his own water.

Rathlin sat and looked at his brother in stunned silence, before he asked his next question.

"So why all this mystery?" pointing to Finian's garb.

"Well my other clothes were blood stained, so I used some blankets I had with me to make this and then when I did get some more clothes from one of the local villages...

well this just seemed more comfortable," he looked at Rathlin. "You know I truly didn't think you would miss me... I knew you would inherit the estate and believed that you would be happy with that..."

"I am sorry I didn't reply to you dear brother, you cannot know how much I regret our impasse," said Rathlin sombrely.

"You have no need to apologise to me Rathlin... it is I who should apologise to you," The Watcher replied, with a tear in his eye. "All these years I never thought you understood the Tek families' obsession with dragons... our ancestors and my life's work... I was truly amazed to hear your name mentioned when Angus and Pyrra first came to Krubera, and even more surprised to learn that you were now head of the revived Secret Society of Dragon Protectors," he smiled warmly at his brother. "I didn't know what to make of it at first, but when you came to see Ward Barfoot and I saw for myself how you had changed, I knew then that father had been wrong to exclude you from the family secret all those years ago. We both misunderstood you. I would have been delighted to have you by my side dear brother... In fact I could have done with your help too, Angus" he said, causing the lad to blush. "My apologies, I have gone on somewhat... What did you come to ask me about?" he asked, looking from one to the other.

Angus now felt as though he was intruding in the brother's reunion, but he had to find out what he came for in the first place.

"Finian, did you remove the wedge from the tunnel roof support?" asked Angus dubiously.

"Indeed I did not... I was trying to figure that one out myself," he replied indignantly, "It was definitely removed on purpose though... I found it lying some yards away... I just can't believe anyone would do such a thing!" he said.

"Did you see who was left in the tunnel?" probed Angus.

"Well let me think now... Almost half the dragons had past me before I left the opening where the wedge was, but I think Pyrra, Godroi... Felspar... Macklin... Farrel and of course poor Cyru," he replied.

"Well at least that narrows it down a bit," added Rathlin. Angus sat deep in thought and felt he needed to speak to Georgina and Rathlin, but only after the head of the SSDP had caught up with his brother.

"Hopefully we can find out who did before someone else gets hurt," he said, "I think I'll go to bed now and leave you two to catch up."

He bade the brothers goodnight and left them alone, but not before returning Rathlin's Dragonore to him from beneath the rock.

"You must tell me what you have been doing these past three years and how you managed to re-build the SSDP so brilliantly," said Finian to Rathlin, as Angus withdrew smiling.

## Chapter 17

# *'Lightning Cheats'*

At first he thought it was Pyrra, but it was a male dragon standing before him, just as it had done the night before. Angus had learned many things about dragons over the past year, and one he knew, was how to tell a male dragon from a female. For a start, the males had more horns on their head and were more whiskey than the females. The scales were the wrong shade as well, being a darker green than Pyrra; in fact this dragon was almost blue. If it were not for the colour and the horns it could have been Pyrra, as the resemblance was very striking. Angus woke up confused and sat bolt upright in his sleeping bag. Perhaps this dragon was one of Pyrra's distant relatives from the past and his close proximity to the Cor Stan was playing tricks on his mind. After all he had been getting some very strange and powerful dreams prior to finding Ward Barfoot. The thought was purged as Rathlin walked in.

"My dear boy, how are you this fine morning?" he asked, looking as if he was ready to jump for joy and click his heels.

"I'm fine… did everything go okay with Finian?" Angus asked, pushing the dream from his mind.

"Wonderful… In fact, he wants to see you before Ward Barfoot calls us to the next Trial," he answered, "We can see him after breakfast, if that's okay with you?"

"No problem!" replied Angus, wondering what the former head of the Society could possibly want with him.

During breakfast they spoke again about the cave-in and tried to work out who could have caused the tunnel to collapse. Both wondered why on earth they would want to do such a thing in the first place.

"But why attack you and Cyru?" pondered Angus thoughtfully, after finishing off some sausages cooked on his stove.

"I don't know lad… maybe I upset someone," he had just cleared his own plate, "Macklin!"

"What about him," queried Angus?

"I was arguing with him after our heat, remember? He almost put us out and I gave him a piece of my mind!" he said emphatically.

"Do you really think he would do that after a little argument?" replied Angus, unsure it was really enough to provoke such a violent response.

"Well maybe you're right... but you saw how he was at The Gathering, he's a hot head and who knows what he would do to win!"

Angus was about to say that maybe Cyru was not the real target but just then Finian walked in and removed his hood as he entered.

"Good morning my dear brother, I hoped you slept well..." he said clapping Rathlin on the shoulder, "and Angus my boy... I said last night that I could have done with your help but according to my brother here, it is you I have to thank for restoring the SSDP and for bringing Rathlin back to me... Indeed without your insatiable appetite for finding answers, none of this would have happened," he took Angus' hand and shook it enthusiastically, "Thank you!"

Angus did not know what to say or where to look, as he was so embarrassed by the praise he received and as usual, he felt he did not really deserve it.

"After talking long into the night, Finian and I agreed to put the past behind us, although he wishes to remain living here, secretly amongst the dragons..." said Rathlin recognising Angus' usual discomfort and modesty, "and therefore remain dead to the outside world... The difference now is he will keep in touch and work closely with us for the good of dragons as the need arises."

"I am completely at home here in the Krubera caves, and now that Rathlin will be sending me some supplies, I can continue my role, staying on after the Trials and assisting the new Guardian" he smiled. "In a little more comfort, I can prepare the caves in readiness for the end of The Great Hibernation."

"The Hibernation is coming to an end?" queried Angus excitedly.

"Yes it must... That is why Barfoot tried to awaken them all... It is now too dangerous for them to continue sleeping and with our help a new generation of dragons will once more inhabit the earth."

Angus was not sure what he meant by all of that, but the conversation was cut short as Georgina popped her head into the cave and this triggered Finian to replace his hood.

"I need to go now as Barfoot will be looking for me," and with a light hearted wave he swept past a very confused looking Georgina.

"Was that the same person?" she asked with a bemused expression.

Angus and Rathlin brought Georgina up to speed on the previous night's events, which took a long time as she constantly interrupted them with one of Angus' favourite sayings. 'No way'!

Soon Angus stood by the mirror pool, with Pyrra and the remaining participants, where they awaited Barfoot's explanation of the next task. There were just half of the original contenders left in the Trials and he had to try and re-focus himself for the task ahead. Everyone in the cavern buzzed in anticipation and an instant hush descended as Barfoot walked in with the hooded Finian at his side.

"So my freonds we find ourselves upon the third task…" he surveyed the small gathering, "A Ward may be called upon to use the weather to their advantage, so he or she must have a complete understanding of how to harness the forces of nature."

Angus looked at Chad and Macklin. He still speculated on whether they could be responsible for the cave-in and what they might try next.

"Tonight we will play host to a weather phenomenon not unknown in these mountains…" he looked upwards at the cavern ceiling, "An impending storm, which you have to deal with, will be at its zenith early tomorrow morning and your task will be to harness some of its energy."

The hooded figure of Finian, stepped forward, and handed what looked like an over-sized crystal ball to the Ward before he stepped back again.

"You will have to make your way into the tempest to capture, and bring back, lightning energy in this glass orb... Your protector will hold it!" the contestants grew restless as he expanded, "Protectors, you will be wearing heavy duty rubber gauntlets to protect yourselves."

With the task explained Barfoot suggested that they all went to rest and mentally prepare for the Trial ahead. They broke off to their caves and each pair debated the task as they went. The protectors were extremely nervous, none of them had ever been exposed to a lightning bolt before, let alone tried to contain one! Knowing that they would have a very early start, some of the protectors tried to take a nap after lunch, but no-one got much sleep due to nerves. That afternoon many theories were discussed on how they could catch the lightning but it was clear that no-one really knew what was in store for them. One by one the humans and the dragons made their way to bed in an attempt to get some sleep before the big event.

It was early dawn and the remaining five dragons made their way out of the entrance of the cave system and onto the bleak mountainside. Gathered outside in the gloom, Barfoot addressed the five teams once more. All were drenched in rain that seeped into Angus' skin, even though he was wrapped up like an Eskimo.

"As you can all see the storm is already raging around us," he boomed, trying to be heard over the howling wind and rain, "The lightning will start soon and you must prepare yourselves to be brave and overcome your fears!" Thunder rumbled in the distance and echoed a warning to the contestants of the impending strikes headed in their direction. Any thought of cave-ins were forgotten and each of them concentrated on the grim, and surely most dangerous, task yet before them. Angus rubbed his sleepy eyes and blinked at the heavens as the rain hit his face. The darkened dawn sky gradually being swallowed by the even darker clouds fascinated him as they gathered in greater numbers and crashed into each other to echo and rumble along the mountain range. Finian passed out the gauntlets and each protector put them on in readiness for the globes. The balls were made of thick glass about the size of a football and Angus clutched it to his body. He feared the possibility of it slipping from his grasp and with Pyrra's help he carefully climbed onto her back. Suddenly the very ground they stood on vibrated beneath them as a boom, so loud it made them all jump, emanated all around them and almost caused Angus to drop his precious sphere. He recovered his composure just before the first bolt of electrical energy discharged from the clouds and arced itself to a rock face roughly one hundred metres above them. His eyesight was drawn unwillingly to the glare of the blue white light and left Angus temporarily blinded. Pink lights danced before his eyes and Angus glanced around at the others trying to regain the focus of his eyesight. Another violent clap of thunder resonated around the clearing, quickly followed by another bolt of electricity. It was a little bit nearer than the last one and fear etched on all of the protectors' illuminated faces.

The Watcher waved them into the maelstrom and all five flew in formation towards the place where the last lightning strike, had lit up the sky. The dragons scaly faces were set in grim determination as they broke formation, each chose what they felt, was the best position to try and capture the elusive phenomenon. Angus looked around and could see only three dragons ahead of him, Godroi

with Georgina, gripping the orb awkwardly; Macklin being
ridden by Chad, who had tucked the orb inside his jacket
for safekeeping; and Nehebkau with Kadin, who fought to
keep hold of the slippery sphere. As Angus watched the
clouds thrash around them, Godroi suddenly disappeared
from sight and at first he assumed that the golden dragon
has passed into a cloud. Then Macklin, who was quite
close, vanished before Angus' eyes. After a few seconds of
confusion Pyrra turned her head and shouted, 'hold tight',
before she switched both of them into dragon time. Angus
watched as both Macklin and Godroi re-appeared magically
a little further away. The rain slowed down as if frozen in
mid-air and Angus could see the same blurring that
occurred during the race at Calmor. They fought to hold a
position amongst the battering winds and it was not long
before Nehebkau joined them to await the next strike.

Angus scanned the clouds to look for Felspar and after
glancing over his shoulder, he assumed the black dragon to
be too far away to see his dark body silhouetted against the
threatening clouds. They continued to gain height until they
were deep inside the storm cloud and Angus could feel his
hair being statically charged as the next build up of energy
took place. Suddenly he felt himself being lifted by one leg

and lurched over unexpectedly, as he had been pushed from underneath. Pyrra turned her head back towards him and banked to keep him in the saddle. As she did so, both could see that Felspar had come up from underneath on Pyrra's blind spot, lashed out at Angus and unhooked his leg from the loop of the saddle. Angus grabbed for the pommel to steady himself and watched in horror as the orb slipped from his grasp. He quickly regained his foothold in the saddle and managed to deal with Pyrra's sudden banking manoeuvre. He even noticed that Fergus seemed unconcerned about Angus' plight at the hands of Felspar, as the older lad held tightly to the black dragon's reins, focused on the path of the lightning ahead. Angus sensed Pyrra wants to give chase and exact revenge for the unprovoked attack, but he reminded her of more pressing matters.

"The orb!" he shouted, alerting her to dive for the sphere before it hit the ground and shattered, thus disqualifying them.

Fortunately she heard him above the din and Pyrra curbed her anger as she went into a vertical nosedive and spiralled down after the orb with her ears back. Angus lay flat along her body, a manoeuvre they had perfected in training. He watched as she hurtled at the ground and he used all his strength and willpower to stay in the saddle. Luckily, despite the head start the thick glass ball had on them, they managed to quickly gather enough speed to catch up and swoop underneath the plummeting globe with only metres to spare. Angus retrieved it and gripped the slippery glass tightly to his body. Dragon time had given them the precious advantage they needed to avoid certain disaster.

Pyrra started to make her way back to the lightning flashes above and she beat her wings relentlessly in an effort to complete the task before the storm passed. Angus was so surprised by the viciousness and stealth of Felspar's attack, that he now had doubts about the cave-in, and who had caused it. He abruptly discarded the thought as his concern grew for the others who were still unaware of Felspar's intent to seemingly win at any cost. He gazed upwards into the heart of the storm. Angus could see the shapes of three dragons and realised that Felspar was not one of them. Frantically Angus scanned the darkened sky for any sign of the dragon's dark body. He hoped that they could reach the others before Felspar succeeded in unseating one of them.

Lightning arced across the sky once more; Angus saw Godroi swivel and Pivot into one of the forks. The bolt disappeared and the gold dragon plummeted downwards  with a frightened, but delighted, Georgina holding the now glowing sphere. Another strike left Chad and Macklin heading home with their prize intact. Angus felt Pyrra turn to head for the point of their success, hopefully to intercept the path of the next lightning strike. He could see Nehebkau just ahead and then Felspar came out of a black cloud directly underneath Kadin. Angus bellowed at them in warning, but they were too far away to hear him amid the cacophony of crashing noise that surrounded them. Pyrra and Angus were helpless spectators as, just at the moment another lightning bolt struck, Felspar flew into Nehebkau and knocked the Egyptian dragon so hard that the jolt reverberated through poor Kadin and forced him to drop his orb.

At first Nehebkau spun out of control unable to regain his composure immediately. This gave the falling sphere too much of a head start. Eventually he dived headlong, just as Pyrra had done, and managed to rapidly gain ground on the globe. But it was all in vain, as he did not have Pyrra's turn of speed and could not quite make it in time. They could only watch in horror as the glass shattered into a thousand fragments on the rocks below. Angus returned his gaze to the body of the dark cheat and, with some pretty deft flying, Felspar managed to get into the path of the lightning that Nehebkau had aimed for. Fergus captured the bolt as he held the orb above his head. He gripped the dragon with his knees and the third orb sped downward to the other two glowing brightly below. Pyrra pushed upward as already the thunder grew more distant and she chased the lightning before it moved on.

"Can we catch it?" shouted Angus leaning as far forward as the orb allowed.

She did not answer him but he could feel her body shudder as the green dragon beat more determinately to an area of cloud that had started to glow with the build up of electrical charge.

"Get ready!" cried Pyrra over her shoulder.

Angus swallowed back his terror as a bolt of lightning that would normally be moving too fast to see properly, now seemed to twist and arc its way to them like some sort of live animal. Pyrra stopped in mid-air, adjusted her wings and body, as she tried to line up in the path of the approaching electrical energy. It was up to Angus now and he had to keep very wary and hold the orb into the path of the bolt. He could not drop it, whatever happened. One false move and he could be struck by the full force of the lightning. He watched in terror as the bolt forked at the last minute and headed directly at Pyrra's body. She did not have much time to think and reacted instantly. Pyrra flicked her wings and twisted her body in mid air. Angus still had the orb in his outstretched hands as he dug his feet into the loops and gripped with his legs as the dragon's violent manoeuvre threatened to throw him from the saddle. The fork was now behind his head and just in time he leaned backwards. The globe took the place of his skull and the electrical energy produced a blinding light that forced him to shut his eyes tightly, but they had the prize they needed.

They continued to twist violently sideways to avoid being electrocuted by the full force of the other fork and Angus blindly clung on for all he was worth. Through the protective gloves, he could feel the angry heat from the captured lightning as if it raged at being trapped in a glass prison. He pulled himself forward again, helped by Pyrra's dive earthwards in her effort to extract them from the storms fury as quickly as possible. Angus had to turn away and shield his eyes from the spheres glare. The orb shone brightly, like some sort of angry mini sun. He kept his hands tightly round it and his face buried in Pyrra's scales as the pair made their way back to terra firma and the safety of the caves. The third and most taxing Trial so far, was safely over.

## Chapter 18

# *'True Colours'*

As the hooded figure of Finian led the irate Pyrra and Angus back into the cavern, they told Georgina and Godroi what had taken place during the Trial. The others had gone on ahead and now stood with Ward Barfoot and a dejected looking Kadin. The Ward waited by the mirror pool, but before he could say anything, Angus, bursting with anger and the injustice of it all, launched straight into a verbal attack on the loathsome actions of the black dragon.

"Nehebkau and Kadin are out of the Trials!" shouted Angus furiously, "We saw it all… You cheated!"

Before anyone realised his intentions Angus ran straight at Fergus, caught the larger boy unaware, and managed to push him over. The taller lad tripped on a rock and fell back into the mirror pool, disturbing the flawless reflection of the small underground lake. Several hands pulled Angus off the stunned and drenched figure of Fergus.

"Angus what's all this about?" demanded Rathlin keeping a firm grip of the lads collar.

"They forced Kadin to drop his orb!" shouted Angus.

Everyone turned to stare at the accused pair and waited on their reply.

"Complete nonsense..." replied Felspar haughtily, "We were simply going for the same lightning strike and unfortunately got in each others way... completely unintentional ... ask Fergus!" he finished, turning to his protector who still looked shaken from Angus' surprise attack.

"Yes... yes it was an accident..." Fergus said meekly.

"How could it be an accident when it happened twice?" spat Angus in reply, "You tried to knock me off as well..."

"Nonsense..." barked Felspar in return, "You would do well to watch who you accuse!" he snarled.

"What do you mean by that?" growled Pyrra stepping forward as she squared up to the larger black dragon. All present, including those who had not taken part in the Trial, had heard the malice in the voice of Felspar.

"Angus!" implored Kadin interrupting the tense atmosphere, "I thank you for your remonstrations on our behalf, but Nehebkau and I accept our fate. We do not wish to see you hurt, or disqualified... Please my friend..." he finished putting a calming hand on Angus' shoulder, "We are unhurt and we thank you for your efforts, but it is not our destiny to continue in the Trials."

"Wise words!" added Barfoot stepping between the posturing pair of Pyrra and Felspar, "Fighting will resolve nothing and cheating is not a worthy attribute of a would-be Guardian. If any such action could be proven then it will be severely dealt with!" he glowered at Felspar as he said the last few words and this seemed to force the dark beast to back down.

Fergus looked at Georgina and could see she was less than impressed with his actions. He decided to try and win some favour back.

"Look, we're sorry if we caused anyone to drop their orb but let's face it, the rain made them slippery and I can assure you, any contact was purely accidental" he said contritely and looked to Felspar for some support.

"All part of the competition if you ask me," the black dragon growled, adding, "To the victor, the spoils!" as he swished his mighty tail and swaggered off full of arrogance and self-importance. "Get over it!"

Fergus just shrugged as if to say 'I tried' and then ran off to catch up with his unruly charge. Angus noticed that Chad and Macklin hurried after them and Angus could not help but think of an old saying his Gran used to say... 'Birds of a feather flock together'.

As some of the others started to filter back to the sleeping caves Angus approached Ward Barfoot to appeal for fair play.

"...after all it was not Nehebkau and Kadin's fault. They were the victims!" he finished pleadingly.

"Angus I know how you must feel... when a wrong deed is done it should not go unpunished, but I have no proof and I will not change the rules" replied the Ward, not without sympathy but with a kind of finality in his voice. Angus stood helplessly as the Ward retired to his quarters, The Watcher at his side.

"It sounds like he is condoning winning by any means..." said Angus dejectedly, "You'd better watch your back Georgina."

"I think it's you who will need to watch yours now" she replied.

"Angus you know it's not smart to argue like that with a boy larger and older than you... Or his huge dragon for that matter!" said Rathlin, trying to keep a straight face. Angus had still not fully calmed down and was not ready to see the funny side, still upset at the unfairness of the situation. It seemed to him that Felspar would stop at nothing to make sure he would win.

It took Angus sometime to settle down and even then the mere sight of Felspar only served to infuriate him, fortunately both culprits stayed inside their own quarters and did not allow Angus the opportunity to confront them again. He was disappointed that, after he explained to Finian exactly what had happened during the storm, the former head of the SSDP was not as outraged as Angus had expected him to be. Instead The Watcher just shrugged and conceded that these things happened and Angus should not get too worked up about it. Rathlin was the only one who shared his conviction of Felspar's guilt as even Georgina wanted Angus to make his peace with Fergus. She tried to convince him that the black dragon's protector was not in control of the rogue's actions. The next morning Angus decided he would seek out the older lad and apologise for attacking him, but before he had a chance to do so, everyone was called to a meeting to discuss the next Trial.

"We now find ourselves faced with the penultimate task," Barfoot said, as he surveyed the remaining competitors before him. "Your next Trial is a real test of your mental abilities…"

Angus looked over at Fergus and Felspar as they listened intently to the Wards explanation. He wondered if he would get a chance to speak to the lad alone.

"…both dragon and protector have to escape… is that clear?" finished Barfoot smiling.

It was not clear to Angus, as he had not listened and he stood looking confused. It took a brief, and hushed, explanation from Pyrra to bring him up to speed on the details he missed through his lack of concentration, but basically it involved the four remaining contestants being placed in a cave with two openings. One was in the ceiling and the other in the far wall. The Watcher had arranged so that he could begin to flood the cave with water after five minutes and Barfoot had explained that it would only take the same time for the cave to flood. If the contestants had not managed to escape through the way out before the water filled the cave, they would be forced to use the entrance and would be disqualified.

Soon Pyrra and Angus were taken with the others to the cave in question and he found himself looking up at Barfoot through the hole in the ceiling they had just entered through. Finian stood beside a makeshift sluice gate that held back the water and stopped it from running into their cave and filling it too early. Angus could already see water as it trickled through and formed small rivulets which ran into the cave they now stood in. As he glanced around it was obvious that the cave was usually filled with water and that it's natural course was through their only allowable exit; a small tunnel barely big enough for a protector to crawl through let alone a dragon. Angus racked his brain in thought. 'There must be some way of doing this that will allow a full sized dragon to pass through that small space. Lateral thinking, that's what was needed.'

"What do you reckon Pyrra?" he whispered.

"I don't know Angus… perhaps if I could morph…" she replied.

It did not look good and Angus judged by the expression on the others' faces that they had not had much luck in coming up with any ideas either. A movement above them caught their attention and they all watched in dismay as the hooded figure of Finian began to open the sluice gate, allowing the water to pour through. 'Surely that could not have been five minutes, I need a way to get Pyrra out of here!' thought Angus as he looked dejectedly at a small

piece of wood that had just begun to swirl around his legs.
Of course! Pyrra had the answer all along! She could
morph into an inanimate object, especially if it was vaguely
dragon shaped!

Angus had no time to explain to the bemused Pyrra as
he picked up the piece of wood and retrieved his penknife
from his trusty backpack. He started whittling and finished
his rough sculpture, whilst he quickly, and quietly,
explained his plan to Pyrra. She had to morph into the
roughly hewn wooden dragon shape and he threw the stick
on the ground.

She did not need to be told twice! The water had risen
rapidly and had already covered most of the cave floor to
make pools in the uneven rock. Pyrra morphed into the
wood, Angus scooped it up and placed it in his backpack.
He glanced encouragingly at Georgina before he quickly
scrambled up to the small pot hole and crawled through as
quickly as he could. Back in the cave the water still rose
and was now at knee height.

"I can't swim!" shouted Chad to Macklin more loudly than he meant to in his rising panic.

"Find me something to morph into then!" snapped the red dragon unsympathetically.

Georgina had seen Angus lead the way; already she had a plan and smiled confidently as she whispered to Godroi. All the while she fingered the dragon brooch pinned on her jacket, given to her by her father. The water continued to rush in and the noise of the water had started to take over as it made its way higher and higher to the small shaft that led to refuge and victory. Fergus and Felspar were deep in conversation as they looked at something Fergus had hidden in his hands. Georgina held up her brooch to Godroi and two of the remaining three dragons simultaneously disappeared. Both Georgina and Fergus waded to the exit with the water now at waist height. The tall dark haired lad made a show of gallantry, allowing her to go first.

"After you madam," he said in a mock posh voice.

"Why thank you kind sir," she replied, mimicking him. Fergus followed Georgina and squeezed himself through the tunnel. Both of their dragons were morphed and safely with them.

Angus climbed out of the tunnel and found himself in a chamber gouged in the middle by the water that had flowed through it. At least until it was recently diverted. Barfoot stood with the contestants already eliminated from the Trials and eagerly waited to greet those who were able to make it through.

"Angus! It pleases me so to see you climb through this opening," said Barfoot, as the damp lad dropped to the floor.

"Thanks!" he grinned, before reaching into his backpack and placing the crude carving on the floor in front of the Ward.

Pyrra morphed to full form in front of the assembled spectators to great applause and cheers. Angus stepped forward and retrieved the small piece of wood as a memento, before being slapped heartily on the back by an immensely pleased and proud Rathlin. Kadin and the others congratulated Angus on his quick thinking, as Pyrra explained to them, 'it was his idea to use the wood and make a sculpture'. The sound of running water interrupted them and Angus turned with the others to see it flow from the small tunnel. His concern mounted for Georgina but soon turned to elation as her head appeared through the opening. She finished pulling herself through and a very happy but bedraggled girl dropped to the floor. Fergus followed and jumped to the floor behind her, equally as soaked, but instead of looking happy he seemed to be troubled. Angus resisted the temptation to run forward to help Georgina, as she struggled up the slope of the worn rock floor. He watched as she triumphantly placed her brooch on the floor at Ward Barfoot's feet.

"Godroi... You can come out now!" she called to the brooch.

Georgina and the assembled crowd were greatly surprised when Felspar sprang out of her brooch first, followed by a rather huffy Godroi who felt his vehicle of choice had been inappropriately commandeered.

"But... wha... you're not supposed to be..." she looked at Fergus, "No you can't!"

"I'm sorry Georgina... it wasn't my idea..." pleaded Fergus.

"No! It was mine... and there is nothing in the rules to say I could not hitch a ride," interrupted Felspar haughtily. "I did not enjoy sharing either, but my necessity was of more importance than my comfort," he said before he flexed his wings and moved off to a corner of the cave away from the growing protests.

Felspar had forced his way into Georgina's brooch at the same time as Godroi and left Fergus to wonder what to do when everyone realised what his partner had done. He had played his part by pretending to have something in his hands. Georgina had not noticed her brooch carried an extra passenger and she was plainly incensed and felt rather used. Soon the water from the opening had increased dramatically and a free flowing stream now ran through the cave. It was obvious that Chad was not going to make it through, which was confirmed when The Watcher entered from another cave, followed by the rather sodden looking young man and his irate partner. Now two arguments were in full swing. On one side of the cave, Chad explained he was not a very good swimmer and, in his panic, he could not think of anything for Macklin to morph into. The red dragon was as usual very angry and arguing back. On the other side, he could see the debate about the use of Georgina's brooch by Felspar had started to get more and more heated. Angus was keen to know what happened to Chad and was secretly pleased that Macklin, the fierce red dragon, was out of the running.

However what grabbed his attention was the argument over the rules of the last Trial.

"How can that be fair?" asked Godroi of Ward Barfoot.

"Well, I have to agree it does not seem fair, but as Felspar pointed out, the rules do not state that it cannot be done…" he said, trying to appease everyone, "I have to let it stand… Felspar was just quick witted enough to seize a chance and use the situation to his advantage."

No-one could really argue and the remonstrations quickly died down. Angus and Georgina were delighted they had got so far in the contest, and had not let Pyrra or Godroi down in any way. The girl had quickly forgotten the hi-jacked brooch and now her eyes were shining brightly with the exhilaration of it all.

"Well done Georgina… it couldn't have been easy climbing through with all that water flooding in," said Angus praising her courage.

"It was a bit scary at first, but I would have been completely stuck in there if I hadn't seen you doing what you did for Pyrra," she gushed. "I can't believe we are both through to the last task!"

Without thinking she jumped at Angus, hugged him, kissed his cheek and made the lad blush profusely. Angus was flustered by the kiss and did not know what to do with himself, but he felt on top of the world. Pyrra delighted in her young protector's embarrassment and she stored the memory away to tease her friend with later.

"So, do you still think I should make my peace with Fergus?" he asked, trying to change the subject and divert everyone from his red face.

"I think you should…" she replied after some thought, "I think it's Felspar that leads him astray and he is just caught up in the middle of it… I guess he is just being loyal to Felspar."

Angus was not so sure that was the case but he agreed that, at the first opportunity, he would apologise for pushing Fergus into the mirror pool. After all it was what Georgina seemed to want and he knew in his conscience it was the right thing to do.

As it turned out, he did not have to wait long for his chance as Felspar and Fergus made their way out of the cave. Angus decided to follow them and speak to the older lad privately. He was about to approach Fergus, when he realised they had walked into a part of the caverns that none of the party had been to before. As usual his curiosity got the better of him and he decided to follow them to find out where they were going. Soon, he found the boy and dragon deep in earnest conversation in a dark corner of the caves and decided that there was no time like the present. He walked towards them with the intention of apologising; however as he approached Angus could not help overhearing what they were saying and he paused to listen.

"The others are becoming suspicious and we'll get disqualified if you're not more careful!" Angus decided to remain hidden as he thought Fergus was obviously telling Felspar his behaviour was unacceptable. He was about to leave and allow the taller lad to chastise the cheating dragon alone, when he heard the reply.

"I don't care about those fools!" spat Felspar venomously.

"But it's becoming too obvious, and you are drawing attention to us… you will give the game away!" pleaded Fergus.

"What are you talking about? I have no fears about that motley crew… they are too thick to associate me with the cave in, and besides, they think it was that stupid Watcher!" replied Felspar.

Angus sank further into the shadows as he could not believe what he heard and did not want to give himself away.

"We are nearly there and all you need to do is keep your nerve for a little longer. When the time is right I will seize the power of that stone one way or another," hissed Felspar arrogantly with a toss of his fierce black head. "I will take care of the girl and as for that boy, he may well end up the same way as Hereward if he dares to stand in my way once more… that's what happens to eavesdroppers!" Angus froze in fear! Was Felspar looking at him? He could feel a pair of narrowing red eyes burn into him as he shrank further into his dark corner. They glinted malevolently and although he felt sure he could not be seen, he was not certain that he had gone un-detected by the power-crazy black beast. Hereward died at the hands of Felspar and Angus had no proof! Now he may be in danger and he feared for his own safety. Unsure of what to do next, Angus slid slowly backwards along the rock wall of the cave until Felspar was out of sight and then kept an eye out behind him, as he made his way back to safety. The first friendly face that Angus found was Pyrra's and he told his dragon friend all that he had overheard.

"What do you think we should do?" he asked.

"Nothing… just yet…" she replied earnestly, "but stay close to me from now on, just in case he tries anything. We need him to make a mistake, some false move that will reveal his true colours. Otherwise, if we challenge him too soon he will just deny it again… Let's wait until an opportune moment and then we will intervene."

## Chapter 19

# 'A Chink in the Armour'

"Wake up sleepy head!" shouted Rathlin into the cave, his voice echoing all around the walls.

Startled into consciousness, Angus jumped up to a sitting position and looked, bleary-eyed, in the direction the voice had come from.

"Am up!" he replied, trying unconvincingly to sound awake.

It had been a fitful night's sleep for Angus, disturbed again by the recurring dream about the familiar looking dragon. He definitely did not recognise him and, having questioned Pyrra several times about her family, he now knew it was not one of her relatives from the past. He had still not told her about the dreams and decided that he would leave it until after the Trials were finished. He got dressed and joined the others in the mirror cave.

"At last," bellowed Hugh Penfold, Georgina's father. "We've been here for ages and I have been dying to hear about your escapades!"

Almost all of the dragons found by the SSDP were in the cavern and this added even more splendour to the normally wondrous sight. Angus could not help thinking, 'this was how the caves would look when they were populated with dragons again'.

"See, I told ya a had a little errand to run!" laughed Liam, as he emerged from behind the Vicar who had arrived, with Argent, for the final Trial and ceremony.

"Awesome!" smiled Angus, as he surveyed the assembled throng.

"So, are ya ready for the final test then?" asked Liam.

"I think so... I just hope that..."

"Best of luck Angus!" said Fergus, cutting him off abruptly.

At first Angus just stood and stared at the outstretched hand of the taller lad, not sure of what to do next. Either Fergus was an extremely cool customer, or he was not aware of Angus' knowledge, from the night before.

"Yeah thanks..." he replied, reluctantly taking the proffered hand, "And you?"

It was obvious that Fergus had not picked up on Angus' unwillingness and Angus guessed that Felspar had neither seen, nor sensed him, the previous night. The large black dragon stood casually to one side of the proceedings, completely aloof, and paid no attention to anyone brave enough to go near him. Angus watched as Fergus continued to shake hands with Georgina, wishing her luck. He began to regret his recent agreement with Pyrra and now he desperately wanted to warn Georgina about the true nature of Felspar, and to tell her that Fergus knew the circumstances of Hereward's death.

"Take care out there," was all he could manage, while he watched Fergus chat to the newcomers, as if completely innocent.

Soon the time arrived for the assembled guests to make way for the three remaining pairs of contestants. Barfoot had cheerfully moved through all the new visitors. He took the time to speak to each in turn, and delighted them with his personal knowledge of their ancestors from thousands of years ago.

"I can't believe he knew my Mother and Father!" said Argent rather impressed and having just met the Ward for the first time.

Barfoot walked towards the entrance of the long tunnel that provided the only way to the surface. He turned slowly to face the assembled guests and commanded an instant silence, with one single look.

"The time has now come, my freonds, for the final task to be performed," he said to the hushed audience, "Soon my time will pass and a new Ward will assume the mantle of responsibility that comes with the title…" he paused to survey the many faces that stared in captivated anticipation, "Guardian of the Cor Stan and keeper of all dragon knowledge, passed from Ward to Ward!"

Angus like the rest hardly dared breathe and he glanced upwards to Pyrra's face wondering if this day would be their last together.

"Would the last three participants please step forward?" he asked.

Each of the pairings began to make their way to the stately white dragon. They weaved through the massed spectators with heads held high. Godroi reached Barfoot with Georgina at his side. Angus and Pyrra joined them and turned to see Felspar arrogantly push past Argent. He forced the silver dragon to side step to catch his balance. If Ward Barfoot observed what happened, he did not let it show and after Felspar had joined them at the front, he began to speak again.

"This final task will take place outside these caves and each contestant will be taken to their starting places, known only to The Watcher and myself," he caught Angus' eye during one of his, now, familiar pauses. "Three dragons have been chosen to escort a contestant to secret locations, and they are not aware of the destinations the others will travel to... Argent, Oswin and Leofric... please join your assigned pairing."

Angus was amused to see that Argent had been paired with Felspar. Both dragons eyed each other malevolently. It was clear neither was pleased about the enforced proximity they would have to endure, during the flight to the starting point of the Trial. Barfoot moved towards the remaining spectators and turned to face the green, gold and black dragons.

"Once you reach your destination, you will be told your next move... The Watcher will inform you when it is time to leave and all that is left for me to do, is to wish you all good fortune," he finished by standing on his hind legs and clapping his fore claws together.

Soon, the others around him began to clap and cheer encouragement and Angus exchanged a nervous smile with Georgina.

"Follow me please!" commanded The Watcher breaking the spell and leading them along the tunnel that led to the surface.

It did not take much time to reach the shimmering wall that magically hid the entrance to the home of The Cor Stan. The hooded figure raised his hand and stopped them short of it.

"Argent, will you lead Felspar to his designated point please!"
As both dragons, and Fergus, passed through the wall, Angus watched and wondered if he would ever get a chance to prove that they had been responsible for the death of Hereward. The thought burned in his head and he felt dismayed as he realised, that by the end of the day, Felspar could be the new Ward. After a few minutes The Watcher indicated that it was Oswin's turn to escort Pyrra, with Angus, to the point they would start the last task. Angus and Georgina wished each other good luck and the solemn trio made their way quietly through the wall, into the darkness beyond. As they climbed, Angus could see daylight and it occurred to him that he had got so used to the suffuse light of the dragon caves, the natural sunlight now seemed harsh and intense by comparison. They soon

stood outside and blinked as they got used to the brilliance of the sunlit mountainside. Snow still capped the peaks, but it was not cold as the light cloud cover, and lack of wind, allowed the sun to bathe them with its rays. They took off and followed Oswin along the mountain. Then they swept left, crossed over the other side of the great peaks and away from the entrance to Krubera. Pyrra trailed closely behind, down into a valley which passed over a small stream and they tracked that for some miles. Unknown to both of them, Godroi and Georgina had already begun their journey to the point they would start the next task. Felspar and Fergus had already reached their destination.

"Well what happens next?" demanded Felspar impatiently.

"YOU have to wait until the messenger gets here!" replied Argent hotly, turning his back on the black dragon.

"MESSENGER... WHAT MESSENGER?" bellowed Felspar infuriated at the over elaborate way the task was being conducted.

"Ha... you'll see!" said Argent almost mockingly as he flapped his wings and left smiling happily at the frustration the black dragon experienced.

Angus watched Oswin fly off into the distance and sat down on a rock to wait for the messenger. He too, was eager to get started and grabbed some stones from the ground and began to throw them at a large rock in the stream. He had just hit the big rock for the eighth time when Pyrra sat up suddenly and caused Angus to drop the stone he was about to throw.

"Someone is coming," she said, stretching her wings outwards as she stood up.

"I thought you were sleeping," replied Angus wondering how she could tell that someone was coming without the Dragonore reacting first.

"I was meditating… here he is now," she replied just as Angus could feel his own Dragonore begin to warm up against his chest."

Angus watched as Gilmor sped into view. The dragon swooped in low and had apparently followed the stream as well. A thought struck Angus.

"Wait… how did you know it was a him?" he asked looking up at Pyrra.

"It's a skill I used to have many years ago but I only just mastered it again," she replied looking rather smug.

Angus wanted to ask her more about this apparently hidden power, but Gilmor deftly touched down beside them and held out an envelope to him. At that very same moment, Nehebkau handed Georgina an identical letter, as was Farrel to Fergus. The tall lad opened it eagerly ripping it apart. He pulled the message from within and began to read.

"The last task is now at hand and you have done well to get this far," he read aloud.

"Power and knowledge await the one who can follow the falling star," said Georgina with Godroi looking on keenly. "Choose your direction carefully, as it will cost you precious seconds," she continued.

"Correctly solve the riddle below and your destiny surely beckons!" finished Angus with a puzzled frown.

"A riddle... I should have known!" growled Felspar with obvious irritation.

"Well come along, read it out to me and let's win this thing," encouraged Godroi enthusiastically.

"All things that start must finish," continued Angus at Pyrra's prompting. "Look to an orbis to see the end."

"The Door you seek will not take war to reach," said Georgina with a thoughtful frown.

"The first one there will claim the prize," intoned Fergus to Felspar. "The new guardian will be named."

"I like the last part, but what did the rest mean?" asked Godroi smiling.

"I don't know," replied Georgina, "but I normally find if I read it over and over again something normally clicks."

"Well, what are you waiting for...hurry up and work it out!" roared Felspar at the visibly intimidated Fergus.

Angus finished reading the riddle for the third time, although this time in his head. He tried to clear his mind and focus on the words before him. Pyrra's head faced the ground with her eyes closed and since she was obviously thinking hard Angus decided to leave her alone with her thoughts. He walked over to a large rock and sat down heavily absorbed in the words. 'All things that start must finish... did that mean the Trials? They had a start and an end. Look to an orbis to see the end... but the orbis was round, a circle and a circle didn't have an end.' Now he was confused. 'Okay what about the next line... The Door you seek will not take war to reach... Well that made no sense... The first one there will claim the prize... The door bit had him stumped, but it was obvious the whole message alluded to a race to a certain place and the first one there would win the Trials. The line before was clearly the key to the location.' He glanced over at Pyrra but she had still not moved from her thoughtful pose. He half wondered if she was sleeping but then another thought struck him. He remembered Miss Puttick and her crossword puzzles and realised that the phrase about the door was a cryptic clue. 'Now how did she do it… sometimes it was a combination of two key words… door and war… the word war definitely was one of them but door could be anything…' Angus scratched his head thoughtfully. 'Why did Door have a capital D?'

"WAR…D!" he said out loud.

Pyrra stirred, opening her eyes and looked at him.

"Have you got it then?" she asked.

"I think so… this line refers to The Ward…' he answered, "I assumed you were thinking about it."

"Me? No… I was dozing… but I knew you would crack it," she smiled knowingly and giving him a cheeky wink, "So what have you got?"

"Well if this is the Ward, then we have to race to him but I'm not quite sure where he is… unless…" he paused evidently thinking.

"What is it?" prompted Pyrra.

"This first bit is a circle, but a circle has no end, or start for that matter…"

"So what does that mean?" asked Pyrra.

"I think it means that you end up back where you started," he looked up at her for some sort of approval.

"Sounds reasonable," she conceded, "So if I understand you correctly, we have to race back to Barfoot and claim the prize?"

"I guess so… but it sounds too easy," replied Angus looking rather disappointed.

"It sounds exactly the sort of thing he would do," laughed Pyrra, "Well, what are we waiting for?" Angus jumped up onto her back and she began to beat her wings with tremendous ferocity and with a few quick strides, launched herself along the stream and back to Krubera.

Georgina had just finished working out the clue with an unconvinced Godroi. The gold dragon did not know Barfoot as well as Pyrra and he was not one hundred percent sure, they were making the right choice by heading towards the caves.

Angus glanced around him scanning the surrounding area for any sign of the others and even though they had gained a little height, as they sped over a nearby summit, he could see nothing. He turned to face forward again and then spun back, as something out of the corner of his eye caught his attention. It was Godroi, as he raced out of another valley, blurring slightly as he used dragon time, like Pyrra. Angus knew Pyrra was just as fast as the male dragon, but Godroi appeared to catch up very quickly.

"Are you okay?" he shouted forward concerned that she may have been ill.

"Of course I am," she replied turning her head to answer, and slowing herself down a little more.
Only when Godroi pulled up alongside her did she seem to flatten her ears to her head and perform at something near her best. Soon Angus heard the familiar golden tones of Godroi as he drew level with them. Georgina hung on determinedly and shouted encouragement to the fired up dragon.

"Why, good afternoon dear lady... A fine day it is for flying... Is it not?" crooned Godroi as he passed Pyrra far too easily.
Angus knew what was going on and understood Pyrra was determined to make sure Felspar did not interfere with Godroi's chances of winning. Georgina smiled and waved

before she pinned her body to help streamline the pair for greater speed.

"C'mon Pyrra let's keep up, you can win this if you want to!" encouraged Angus outwardly, but he knew as well as Pyrra did what winning would mean to their friendship.

Angus leaned forward over her neck and flattened himself as they flew over the top of the mountain. That was when he noticed the shadows on the ground. Three of them! Pyrra slanted her body downwards as they sped down the other side of the mountain, not far behind Godroi. Angus glanced down behind her body and observed that Felspar passed underneath in a blur. At first Angus feared the black dragon was about to try and attack again, but instead Felspar beat his wings harder and stretched looking hungrily at Godroi. Pyrra glanced down and watched for any sign of danger, but it looked as if Felspar was focused only on winning the race back to the caves. Or was he? Angus realised, at the same time as Pyrra, what was going on. Felspar's eyes glinted and were firmly fixed on Godroi's stomach; the vulnerable underside where he had lost a few jewels in the training accident at Calmor. Angus knew instinctively that the black dragon was going to try and wound Godroi in his unprotected weak spot, but before he could shout out, Pyrra reacted. She flipped her body sideways and with a flick of her wings she spun herself downwards. It was all Angus could do to hold on and he held his breath as she skilfully clipped Felspar's left wing and forced him to twist in mid air. Godroi powered on oblivious to the drama that had unfolded behind him. Felspar recovered quickly and tried to continue his pursuit of Godroi but Pyrra changed course and hurled herself at the black beast. She unleashed all her pent up power. Although she was the smaller dragon, she was strong and Felspar reeled away off course in an effort to gain the upper hand with his determined attacker. The enraged black dragon twisted in mid air in an attempt to face Pyrra, his teeth were exposed viciously in a snarl and his tail flicked like a provoked cat. Pyrra undeterred by his angry posture, ploughed head on into Felspar's body. The force threw him backwards into the mountainside and almost crushed Fergus in the struggle. The dark beast grabbed Pyrra by the neck and tossed her sideways, which in turn, tossed Angus from his saddle. He rolled over as he landed he could see Felspar had moved in to slash the green dragon's exposed back with his claws, but before the enraged black dragon reached her, Pyrra flicked her tail upwards and slashed at his face forcing him back. She roared, spun menacingly at her opponent and bore down on him before he could regain the initiative. Felspar was incensed and reared up lashing out at Pyrra, his red eyes full of spite and evil. Angus only realised that Fergus still hung in there, as the tall lad jumped from the back of Felspar and tumbled down the slope in an effort to avoid being crushed by the flailing dragons. Felspar charged again snarling and snapping viciously at Pyrra and managed to corner her by forcing her back into a crevice in the mountainside. Angus thought he was about to see his friend badly hurt or even killed. He looked on in horror fearing the worst for his friend and helpless to aid her. Suddenly Cyru, Argent, Gilmor, Farrel and Nehebkau appeared from nowhere. Charging like the cavalry, they pinned Felspar to the ground and put an end to his vicious onslaught.

## Chapter 20

# *'The New Ward'*

Godroi and Georgina raced towards the entrance of Krubera, the great golden dragon forced every ounce of speed he could, from his wings. The pair had the finish in sight and could see that some of the dragons had already come out to meet them. Godroi mentally prepared himself for the ecstatic welcome that would surely greet him with, but was then surprised as they flew straight past him. Perplexed but not thrown off his stride, he kept up his dive to the finish, swooped down to the entrance and came to a perfect halt in front of Ward Barfoot. The onlookers around the Ward erupted into cheers as they roared and clapped their congratulations.

"Well done Godroi... I am pleased to see you have triumphed and if you will now follow me we shall make preparations for the final ceremony," said Ward Barfoot ushering him into the cave entrance.

"But what about the others?" asked Godroi, looking over his shoulder in his worry, and now concerned for Pyrra and Angus.

"Ah. Do not worry my freond, the others will be along shortly and all will be revealed in good time," replied the Ward sagely.

Barfoot, Godroi, the cheering crowd and a now anxious Georgina, began to make their way into the caves, heading for the Cor Stan.

As the triumphant Godroi made his way into the mountain, the other competitors descended slowly down the mountain to the hollow that marked the entrance to Krubera. Felspar was being roughly escorted by the dragons that had subdued him. Even though he was physically restrained and now faced with too many opponents to overcome, the black dragon still threw malevolent looks behind him towards Pyrra and Angus as they led a fearful looking Fergus at the rear of the party.

Ward Barfoot stood in front of the radiant blue rock and awaited the straggling arrival of the others. Godroi was visibly nervous as he restlessly paced behind the Cor Stan. He wished the others would hurry up. It was not his desire to become Ward that made him uneasy but the uncertainty of not knowing what had become of Pyrra. Just as he thought this, Argent appeared with Nehebkau and Gilmor, between them they escorted a furious Felspar.

"I demand justice!" roared the black dragon as he was physically dragon handled towards the Ward.

"Justice for what?" asked Barfoot calmly.

"This cheat attacked me as I was about to pass Godroi and ruined my chances of winning!" accused Felspar, pointing at a serene looking Pyrra as she entered the cave behind the others.

"This is a serious accusation Pyrra... Do you deny this deed?" pressed Barfoot.

"No I don't!" she replied calmly, "I did attack him!" The dragons and protectors around the cave gasped in amazement at this shocking news, but Barfoot looked her in the eye.

Thinking he had the upper hand, Felspar bellowed triumphantly.

"YOU SEE... I demand that the last Trial be repeated between Godroi and me!"

"I would like to hear why Pyrra attacked you?" replied Barfoot, "I am sure she must have had good reason," he said looking back to her.

A hushed silence fell upon the assembly as all attention focused on Pyrra. Angus stood resolutely beside her. He looked up at her and she turned her proud head to face him. She gazed into her young protector's blazing eyes and knew beyond any doubt that she had done the right thing. Their destiny lay together, of that she was certain.

"I had the greatest of reasons…" she said, looking up at Barfoot, "I could not allow this wretched beast to kill another dragon!"

Voices shouted and roared with disbelief and protest throughout the cave, none more vocal than Felspar, who was once again determinedly restrained by his captors. Pyrra did not move a muscle as she stood and stared the black dragon in the eye.

"Please explain your statement," prompted Barfoot seriously.

"This despicable being before you was about to attack Godroi by slashing at the weak spot in his jewelled armour…" again a buzz rose around the cave, "I intervened to stop him and he turned on me. If it had not been for the others, I have no doubt he would have killed me also!"

"We could see the battle and that is why I sent the others to put an end to your struggle... but tell me what other dragon you refer to?" the old Ward asked soberly.

"Why, Hereward!" replied Pyrra turning her head to look at Felspar, "He killed Hereward by throwing him down that crevice at Calmor!"

The entire assembly was stunned into silence and some stared open mouthed in horror at Felspar.

"This is madness... why would I kill a blind old dragon?" mocked Felspar.

"I do not know perhaps because he heard something he should not have, but it did not stop you bragging about it, or stop you causing the cave in for that matter..." countered Pyrra.

"How dare you accuse me..." spat Felspar.

"YOU... have constantly cheated your way through these Trials and will stop at nothing to get what you want!" answered Pyrra, fervently raising her voice to match the expostulating dragon.

"I will not listen to these lies... they are a deranged dragon's excuse for attacking me without reason and I demand justice!" growled Felspar as he turned beseechingly towards the many dragons and protectors assembled in the cave.

The place went into tumult as everyone shouted and conjectured at the same time. Angus glanced at Barfoot and wondered how the white dragon would sort this out. Would he believe Pyrra? He did not need to wait long for an answer.

"Order… please… everyone calm down…" said the Ward as he turned to face Pyrra once more, "Pyrra do you have any proof of these serious charges you have brought on Felspar?"

Pyrra shook her head and the noise started up again. Angus could see that Felspar grinned triumphantly at Pyrra and he decided he could not standby and watch any longer.

"Ask Fergus!" he shouted at the top of his voice.

His cry was all but lost in the uproar and the arguments continued on as if nothing had been said, but Godroi and Ward Barfoot had heard his demand. Angus moved to Fergus and stood in front of him.

"I said ASK FERGUS!" he bellowed at the top of his voice and finally gained the attention of everyone in the room.

"Leave him out of this!" growled Felspar menacingly.

Ward Barfoot stepped between the black dragon and Fergus, and shielded the boy from the black dragon's view.

"Fergus will you answer the accusations?" asked Barfoot quietly.

Fergus looked up awkwardly into the compelling face of the Ward and nodded hesitantly.

"Did Felspar have anything to do with the cave-in?" he asked.

At first Fergus said nothing and just stared at the ground, unable or unwilling to answer. Angus felt enraged and wanted to lash out at the taller lad, such was the strength of ill feeling he felt towards him for being part of Hereward's sad demise.

"We must have an answer?" asked Barfoot patiently.

Fergus hesitated for a moment and then he mumbled.

"Yes, he caused it…"

"BE QUIET YOU FOOL!" roared Felspar, struggling to free himself from his restraining captors.

Fergus backed away from Felspar now afraid of the black dragon's wrath.

"You need not be frightened Fergus… I will not allow you to be harmed," assured Barfoot, "Tell us what happened to Hereward?"

"I didn't know he was going to kill him… he just told me to go and that he would take care of him… I didn't think he would kill him!" blurted Fergus as Felspar roared and struggled.

"He didn't kill him right away…"replied Angus, "He threw him down that dark hole to die slowly and cruelly!"

"I didn't know, I swear I didn't know…" pleaded Fergus, "I only found out this week how he died… I wanted to stop before someone got hurt and that's when he told me it was too late to worry about that!"

"I should have thrown you down that stinking hole as well, you spineless insect!" howled Felspar, straining to get loose.

"ENOUGH OF THIS!" commanded Barfoot, "You can go nowhere and I will not let you harm another being… not even a fly!"
Felspar seemed to shrink as the Ward's stature grew above him, forcing the black dragon into acquiescence. Evidently Barfoot had more power than he had made openly apparent, although Angus noticed that the Ward looked more tired than he had seen before.

With Felspar subdued it was not long before they managed to coax the rest of the story from Fergus. He confessed to the cave-in; Felspar's role in the unfair disqualification of Nehebkau and the attempt on Godroi's life. By this time the place was in a complete frenzy, as humans and dragons expressed everything from disgust to vehemence. Fergus cowered in the face of the insistent calls for Felspar and himself to be punished and Angus was surprised to find himself feeling sorry for the lanky lad. At a nod from Barfoot, Finian moved beside Fergus. The Watcher placed a comforting, but firm, hand on the boy's shoulder as Barfoot turned his attention to Felspar. He pronounced the dragon's guilt.

"Felspar you have brought great shame and dishonour to yourself..." he said sorrowfully, "You have taken the life of another dragon and that is a crime that has not been committed for over eight thousand years. I must punish you but before I do, what have you to say in your defence?" At first Felspar did not answer and stood stock still, held steady by four other dragons. He stared at the floor and it seemed that he had nothing to say at all until. Suddenly he jumped forward and strained against his subjugators. This caused some of the guests to reel back, fearing what he might do in his desperation.

"You ask me to defend myself?" he spat at Barfoot, "I wanted to use the power of the Ward to free dragons! For too long we have hidden from these humans and I would see to it that dragons ruled the Earth once more!" he glared at the dragons surrounding him with eyes that shone blood red, "We have slept too long and this dragon has let our kind dwindle to the verge of extinction!" he glowered at Barfoot accusingly, every part of his being oozing hatred, "I will not defend what I have done and if I had to do it again, I would…"

"ENOUGH!" bellowed Barfoot, forcing Felspar to cower at the ferocity present in the command, "It is obvious to me that you are beyond redemption, but our laws dictate that I cannot take your life," he said, towering over the body of the retreating black dragon. "You will be banished from the Cor Stan Felspar, and the 'Heart Stone' you have, will be taken from you…" Barfoot slashed at Felspar's chest and in one movement he had removed the Dragonore. He held it up as he turned to the others, "Without this, your powers will be harmless. You will have barely enough left to keep you from detection."

The dragons and protectors around the incident began to murmur their approval and at Barfoot's command, Felspar was taken to the far side of the cave.

With the black beast now restrained, everyone soon began to settle down as Barfoot made preparations to give up his powers as Ward and allow Godroi to take up the mantle he had won by right. The golden dragon was somewhat subdued; Pyrra sensed his unease and walked over to speak to him.

"You do not seem yourself Godroi, what is the matter?" she asked.

"I do not deserve to be Ward," he replied forlornly.

"Of course you do. Why would you say such nonsense?" she chided.

"You should have won Pyrra… you could have beaten me but instead you let me win… why?" he pleaded.
She looked at him fondly and smiled.

"I could not stand by and let that brute hurt someone I love and I had already decided that I could not leave Angus," she replied kindly, "I get the strange feeling that he and I have other things to do," she said wistfully.

"But I don't deserve this…" said Godroi dejectedly.

"Don't you ever say that!" replied Pyrra with vehemence, "I believe in you… so much so, I was willing to sacrifice myself, and even Angus, to see you in your rightful place. So do not talk to me of deserving. This is your right and you will be a worthy successor to Barfoot. Of that, Godroi the Golden, I am sure!"

He looked into her face and gained courage from her conviction. Godroi smiled, nodded and addressed her, more like his old self.

"Well, far be it for me to argue with such a formidable lady," he teased, stepping back and bowing towards her, his self confidence seemingly restored.

"Are you ready Godroi?" asked The Watcher, interrupting the golden dragon's theatrics.

Godroi was ushered next to the Cor Stan; he stood on one side and faced Barfoot on the other side. Angus was joined by Pyrra and everyone gathered round eagerly. They waited to see what would happen next and soon the blue stone began to glow and dim in a repetitive and hypnotic way as the Ward closed his eyes and whispered some ancient words in the dragons own language. The radiance of the light lessened and brightened with increasing intensity, until the rock itself was almost too dazzling to look at. Suddenly just as it did in the cavern under Calmor, the blue stone sent out a beam of light directly at Ward Barfoot striking him on the chest. This caused his head to tilt backwards and with his eyes closed, Angus believed he was in pain. The ancient dragon continued to chant the spell that had triggered the Cor Stan to react in the fashion it had. Just as suddenly, a twin beam arced itself from the stone onto Godroi and its power caused him to throw back his head, eyes closed, mirroring Barfoot. Light began to pulsate through the beams from Barfoot to Godroi and Angus watched as everyone around him was immobilised, as if frozen in time. All present stood, mesmerised by the beam of light that joined the two dragons. As he watched the pulse of light, it transferred from Barfoot to the new Ward. Angus realised that all the history, knowledge and power that had been amassed down the ages by Wards since time immemorial, would now become Godroi's.

Barfoot dropped to his knees and Angus was dismayed to see that the Ward was physically shrinking before his eyes. The very life force the stone had given Barfoot to sustain his existence far beyond his natural years, was now being drained away. The once strong and noble white beast now looked ancient and diminished. As suddenly as it had started the beam ceased and Barfoot fell to the ground. Darkness seemed to surround them all. The light blue of the Cor Stan had dimmed to normality and such was it's brightness before that the normal glow now seemed inadequate. Godroi stood exhausted, not only by the enormity of the power transference, but by his efforts during the Trials, and he too, eventually succumbed and slumped to the floor.

## Chapter 21

# *'Misplaced Fragment'*

Everyone stood motionless, stunned by the spectacle they had just witnessed, and taking advantage of his guards' lapse in concentration, Felspar swiftly sprang from the shadows in a last attempt to kill the new Guardian and thus seize all power for himself. Pyrra and Angus were the only ones quick witted enough to react to the attack on Godroi, and once again the brave green dragon selflessly launched at Felspar without thought for her own well-being. Before he could reach Ward Godroi, she stretched her neck forward and with a massive exhalation, breathed fire in the direction of the black dragon and stopped him in his tracks. Caught off guard by the unexpected counter-attack, Felspar checked his run and charged Pyrra instead. The two of them clashed for the second time that day. They viciously snapped at each other, locked in deadly combat. Felspar, once again, threw the slighter dragon against the rock wall of the cave, before he turned to face his intended victim.

Godroi had still not recovered from the transference of power but, sensing he was in grave danger, he tried to get up from the cave floor. Felspar charged at him, just as the new Ward managed to rise. The black dragon grabbed Godroi by the throat and pinned him to the Cor Stan. Felspar roared and laughed mockingly as he raised his right fore claw and prepared to slash open Godroi's exposed neck, thus dealing a killer blow.

"The new Ward indeed!" he sneered.

As his claw swept forward, Pyrra hurled herself into Felspar's body with as much force as she could muster. She knocked him off balance, together with Godroi, and the Cor Stan simultaneously. This caused the stone to dislodge from its position for the first time in several millennia. A number of things then all happened at once. The dragons, that had held Felspar captive, bore down on him once again and forced him to submit to superior numbers. Angus ran to Pyrra's aid, as he could see that she had injured her leg when Felspar had slammed her against the wall. Georgina helped raise Godroi up from the rocky floor of the cave, and Barfoot, with one last effort, raised one claw and steadied the great stone, before he fell back to the ground and exhaled his last breath.

"Are you alright Godroi?" asked Pyrra, picking herself up from the floor and nursing her back leg.

"Yes… and once again thanks to you… but I am afraid Barfoot has gone!" he replied solemnly, looking in the direction of the former Wards prone body. Angus turned sadly to look again on the once proud, but now frail and lifeless body of Barfoot. Just as before when Hereward passed, the body began to glow at the mouth, but this time Angus could not bear to watch. As the ancient white dragon's body incinerated itself, everyone bowed their head in respect. Only when there was nothing, but a wisp of ash rising from the cave floor, did they lift them again. All that remained of the great beast, were the jewels spread on the floor, just as it was with Hereward.

The silence that followed seemed endless, as no-one wanted to break the spell that had entranced them all. It was only when Godroi had fully recovered that things went back to normal. If you could call being in a vast cave system, deep underground in Eastern Europe, with almost thirty dragons and thirty humans normal! Godroi solemnly walked to the scattered stones, and kneeling down, he lay over the spot that Barfoot had occupied only minutes before. When he arose and turned to face the silent onlookers Angus could see that he had replaced the patch of stones missing from his underside, with some of the stones that Barfoot had left behind.

"Such used to be our way, and will be forever more," said Ward Godroi, and turning to Rathlin he continued, "You must scatter Hereward's ashes and jewels here in Krubera, so that others may do the same."

Godroi drew himself up to his full majestic height and Angus was convinced he was larger than before. His first act as the new Ward and Guardian of the Cor Stan, he reinforced Felspar's banishment. He commanded that the black dragon be taken from the Cor Stan's proximity and be forever deprived of its restorative powers. The guards led Felspar away to the caves that housed the contestants. He was to be jailed there until he could be safely escorted from Krubera. Now Godroi had recovered from the power transference, he was quite safe from Felspar and anyone else who might be foolish enough to try and attack him.

Soon congratulations rained down on him, and Godroi revelled in the knowledge he had gained. He could recall facts he had never known before and everyone agreed he would make an excellent Ward. Pyrra and Angus were treated as heroes for saving the new Ward. They took their

leave and returned to the sleeping quarters to allow Angus
to gather his belongings for the long journey home.

They arrived to find Georgina crying while she packed
and Pyrra tactfully whispered to Angus that she would
leave him to deal with this.

"Erm... you okay?" he asked, unsure of what to say. He
instantly regretted such a stupid question.

"I'm fine..." she sniffed, "I just didn't realise until now,
how much I'm going to miss him," she finished looking up at
Angus with wet cheeks.
Without really thinking about it he stepped forward and put
his arm round her as she tried to dry her eyes.

"I don't even know how I am supposed to get home!"
she said, half-heartedly laughing at her own lack of
foresight.

"You can come with Pyrra and me... we'll take you
home," he said without hesitation.

"Will you?" she asked, looking at him through brimming
eyes.

"Yeah... course I...we will," he said smiling, but
blushing in her gaze.

Georgina leaned across and kissed him gently on the lips, an action that caused Angus' insides to flip upside down and inside out all at once.

"Thank you," she replied coyly, but pleased at the same time.

Not only was Georgina delighted that she would return home with Angus, but she was also pleased to accept his further offer to take her out on Pyrra from time to time. At least until the SSDP found her another dragon to protect.

A few hours later the whole of Krubera was assembled in the splendid mirror cave and Godroi stood proudly with The Watcher at his side. Finian no longer wore the hood and most of the guests were very keen to meet the former head of the SSDP as the news spread of his amazing story. Georgina finally released her grip of Godroi and said one last tearful goodbye, before going to be comforted by her father.

"So… are you ready for this?" asked Pyrra.

Godroi looked thoughtful for a few seconds.

"Yes… I think I am… In fact, I never really considered the prospect of not competing and winning was always my goal, but to actually become Ward of all dragons is an

honour I can truly say, suits me!" he smiled, his self belief
fully restored.

"I will miss you but we'll visit as much as we can and I
will bring Argent to annoy you as well" she winked back.
They hugged and Pyrra joined Angus who was saying
goodbye to the Tek brothers.

"Well my boy, you certainly have started something
here… Just look at what the pair of you have achieved,"
said Finian, indicating the many dragons gathered in the
cave.

"Fantastic!" agreed Rathlin, "and now that we have the
Cor Stan, and a youthful new Ward, I have no doubt we will
find even more."

Pyrra placed a gentle claw on Angus' shoulder,
indicating that it was time to go and both said their
goodbyes before they joined Georgina. Finian and Rathlin
embraced as brothers for the first time in many years and
some of the guests started to make their journey home.

"Well Fergus, we'd better get you home," said Rathlin
as he joined Cyru and the others.
Fergus did not answer and instead just hung his head in
shame. Argent had left Gilmor and Farrel to deal with the
troublesome Felspar so he could say his own farewell to his

old friend, Godroi. This left the black dragon with a slim window of opportunity to escape his captives and he did not intend to waste it. He lashed out at Farrel and pushed the two unsuspecting dragons away allowing him to speed for the exit that led to the surface. Before anyone could stop him he disappeared up the tunnel and out of sight. The dragons that remained in the mirror cave, swept after him and by the time they reached the shimmering wall, they found Nehebkau, Leofric and Oswin.

"Did Felspar pass you?" asked Argent, baffled by the dragon's disappearance.

The three dragons indicated that they had not seen him nor heard anything, and if they had, they would certainly have stopped him. They stood guard at the wall and waited for the others to go back through the tunnel. They checked they had definitely not somehow missed a large black dragon. They searched for over ten minutes and gave up believing that Felspar had somehow used dragon time to get past the others. Although the three dragons vehemently denied they would miss a dragon in any form. Disappointed at losing their charge, the dragons returned to their protectors and the last remaining party began the journey down the tunnel. Despite Felspar's escape the mood of the party was very upbeat and they were glad to be going home at last.

"Rathlin, I have to tie my shoe lace… is it okay?" asked Fergus nervously.

"Of course you can lad…" he replied, "You don't have to be so worried Fergus… We all know you were not in control of the situation," he added, suddenly feeling sorry for the boy, "Don't you worry about Felspar… He doesn't have his 'Heart Stone', so he is quite powerless and once I take you home that will be the end of it."

"Th…thanks," he stuttered nervously as he bent down to tie his lace.

The others continued talking until they were interrupted by the sound of moving rocks inside the tunnel. They looked round at Fergus again.

"Sorry… It was an accident," said the frightened lad, indicating a small pile of rocks on the cave floor.

At long last, Angus was back in the air with Pyrra and Georgina happily seated behind him with her arms wrapped around his waist. Argent carried Hugh Penfold, Gilmor and Farrel flew just ahead and Cyru was just behind with Fergus and Rathlin. The errant black dragon was now all but forgotten. Nehebkau had headed south to Dubai and

Oswin flew Northwest with his brother Leofric. All carried their weary protectors back home. They finally arrived back over the British Isles and both Pyrra and Argent dived downwards towards Marnham. They flew around the church house that meant home to Georgina and her father before they landed softly in the garden. The protectors waved at each other as the two groups parted company.

"Thanks for the lift Pyrra… Thanks Angus," said Georgina kissing him on the cheek.

"See you next week?" asked Angus shyly.

"You bet!" she replied enthusiastically before skipping off after her father.

"Do you think we will ever see Felspar again?" asked Angus as they took off for Kynton.

"I sincerely hope not!" Pyrra replied before switching into dragon time.
As she stretched her neck forward to gain speed, she secretly suspected that they had not seen the last of him.

Rathlin headed in the direction of Fergus's home, having left Farrel and Gilmor winging their way back to Dublin. Cyru dropped down into a park and, after taking the coveted Dragonore from a disconsolate Fergus, Rathlin watched the boy walk across the grass and over a footbridge that crossed a dual carriageway on the way to his house. Once he was sure the boy was safely inside Cyru took off for Calmor and the home of the SSDP.

Inside the house, Fergus put his bag on the floor and took off his jacket as he entered the kitchen. As he expected there was no-one at home and he threw the jacket over one of the kitchen chairs. He slumped heavily down into it, folded his arms on the table and rested his head on them. He stayed like this for a few moments before getting up and going outside to the back garden. Fergus placed his hand in his pocket and brought out another piece of Dragonore. It was very small, but it worked and he checked the skies whilst he held it. When he was satisfied that no dragons, nor protectors, were in sight he place his hand into his other pocket and pulled out a pound coin. He played with it for a few seconds and twisted it in his fingers whilst he studied the pictures on both sides. He had picked it up in the tunnel when he stopped to tie his lace and now he threw it into the grass in front of him.

"It's safe... You can come out now," he said to the ground.

Gradually, a dark shape morphed out from the coin on the ground and the unmistakably dark and menacing body of Felspar materialised in front of the tall lad.

"So how did you manage to get away then?" asked Felspar stretching himself.

"They blamed you and said I was just easily led," the lad smiled warily.

"So, the fools don't suspect you helped me escape?" the black dragon sneered.

"No. They thought you managed to sneak past the others using dragon time," replied Fergus shaking slightly.

"Wouldn't they be pleased if they knew that it was precious Angus that gave you the idea for using this coin as a means of escape?" laughed Felspar, "That was a good idea of yours to place the coin in the tunnel... You were correct in thinking I might need it... I thank you for that and I now hold us even."

"Th...thanks... So you are not angry with me,"

whispered Fergus fearfully, as he picked up the one pound coin and looked at the dragon image on the back of it.

"I am still angry with you but you are only human after all, and as I said, you have helped me to escape," replied the dragon coldly.

"What will you do now?" he asked Felspar, wishing the beast would just go and leave him alone.

"I have an idea or two… and with the Dragonore I trapped between my back claws, I will be able to achieve my goal," replied the black beast nastily.

With that said he flicked his wings, launched into the warm August air and flew off over the houses leaving Fergus standing alone on the freshly-cut lawn.

# List of dragons found so far

| | |
|---|---|
| Pyrra | Farrell |
| Godroi | Wolfstanus |
| Argent | Angharad |
| Rhys | Oswin |
| Nathair | Leofric |
| Cyru | Nehebkau |
| Grimbald | Macklin |
| Kendrick | Felspar |
| Hildred | Piran |
| Galfridus | Wyma |
| Swithin | Alwin |
| Sperling | Caedmon |
| Beorn | Radulf |
| Caedmon | Eoghan |
| Walkelin | Hereward |
| Uchtred | Barfoot |
| Gilmor | |

# Lexicon of Old English

| | | | |
|---|---|---|---|
| Ac | - | And | |
| Anginn | - | Beginning | |
| Asmeagan | - | Imagine | |
| Aweccen | - | Awaken | |
| Befeallan | - | Happening | |
| Behealdan | - | Gathering | |
| Biddan | - | Ask | |
| Brengan | - | Brought | |
| Bysen | - | Original | |
| Ceosan | - | Choose | |
| Cumin | - | Come | |
| Cunnan | - | Know | |
| Cynn | - | Kind | |
| Eall | - | All | |
| Efne | - | Only | |
| Forðferan | - | Die | |
| Forstandan | - | Understand | |
| Freonds | - | Friends | |
| Gameatan | - | Dream |
| Gefera | - | Companion |
| Gemunan | - | Remember |
| Halettan | - | Hello |
| Ham | - | Home |
| Hearm | - | Harm |
| Hige | - | Thought |
| Hleo | - | Protector |
| Lange | - | Long |
| Libban | - | Living |
| Mægen, Miht | - | Strength, Power |
| Mæst eðnis | - | Great Comfort |
| Na | - | Not |
| Niwe | - | New |
| Ongytenes | - | Knowledge |
| Rodor | - | Sky |
| Sceawian | - | Looked upon |

# Glossary

**Alter-shell -** An inanimate object in which a dragon hides. The object stays the same even if the dragon is not hiding within it.

**Dragonore -** The precious stone which enables dragons and dragon protectors to recognise each other.

**Dragon time** – A power used by a dragon to speed up or slow time.

**Great Hibernation** – The name used by dragons to describe their enforced hiding until such a time they deem the earth a safe place to once again inhabit.

**Morphing or to morph** – A verb used by dragons to describe their transformation into an inanimate object.

**Heart Stone** – The ancient name given to 'Dragonore'.

Debi Evans is a firm believer in dragons. She originally perceived 'The Dragon's Tale' as a picture book short story for young children until she asked John to illustrate it. In him she found a dragon soul-mate who suggested a better ending, which turned out to be a beginning. The plot grew as ideas flew backwards and forwards into the collaboration 'The Secret Society of Dragon Protectors' has become. The short story was written for her parents; Joan James who would have loved to own the sweet shop and John James who would still bring the oilcan and paint.

John MacPherson lives with his family in Dubai and works far too many hours! Born in Glasgow and working as an engineer in the Shipbuilding / Oil & Gas construction industry for more years than he cares to remember, he did not expect to find himself co-writing and illustrating a children's book. However, after meeting Debi as a leader in the Scout movement, she did the unthinkable and dared to open the door to his imagination. Little did Debi know what she was unleashing and together they have created the fantastic dragon filled world that is the SSDP.

Look out for book three in the series.

# THE SECRET SOCIETY
## OF
# DRAGON PROTECTORS

## 'A Shadow in Time'

For further details visit the official SSDP
website at

www.thesecretsocietyofdragonprotectors.com